Forget Me Not Cowboy

Enemies-to-Lovers Clean Romance Novel

Skylar White

Self Published

Copyright 2024 by Skylar White - All rights reserved.

In no way is it legal to reproduce, duplicate, or transmit any part of this document in either electronic means or in printed format. Recording of this publication is strictly prohibited, and any storage of this document is not allowed unless with written permission from the publisher.

All rights reserved.

Respective authors own all copyrights not held by the publisher.

Contents

1. Prologue — 1
2. Chapter One — 7
3. Chapter Two — 12
4. Chapter Three — 18
5. Chapter Four — 24
6. Chapter Five — 31
7. Chapter Six — 37
8. Chapter Seven — 48
9. Chapter Eight — 56
10. Chapter Nine — 63
11. Chapter Ten — 69
12. Chapter Eleven — 78
13. Chapter Twelve — 90
14. Chapter Thirteen — 96
15. Chapter Fourteen — 102
16. Chapter Fifteen — 110
17. Chapter Sixteen — 114
18. Chapter Seventeen — 120
19. Chapter Eighteen — 127
20. Chapter Nineteen — 135
21. Epilogue — 141

Afterword	146
Also By	147
Also By	149
Also By	151
Also By	153

Prologue

DARLA

It's been a slow, droll, lull of a shift at Our Lady of Peace hospital in Amarillo, Texas—two days before Christmas in fact, and I feel like death warmed over. I've been working doubles for two weeks without a day to myself, and though my feet hurt, and my legs feel weak, I carry on like usual.

I mean, any human being stuck in my position would be exhausted too, so what's the use in whining about it.

It's okay though, I need the money. My husband, Doctor Joseph Middleton, and I not only work at the same hospital, but we own a little farm together. I love all the animals with everything I have. They're like my little babies now that Sparrow and Joe Junior have left the nest, making the place not feel so. . . well. . . empty. The only problem is that nothing in life is free, and the upkeep on the place is expensive enough. But with inflation and the bank increasing our mortgage. . . even between the two of us it's been hard to keep afloat.

So, I suppose it's a blessing that I am getting all these extra hours anyways, though it's not so great for everyone else.

It's flu season here at the hospital, and thanks to the tourists enjoying the warmer weather from up north—and just the time of year in general—it's been making its icky rounds and spreading through the nursing staff like a California wildfire. But call it good diet and exercise or just dumb luck, but I'm one of the few that haven't caught it yet while everyone else is calling out, leaving us incredibly understaffed.

As the night wanes on, however, it's beginning to feel much different than the normal fatigue I've been experiencing. In fact, each step feels heavier than the next, as if my feet have concrete blocks tied to them. I'm dragging them along behind me as I'm finally able to reach the nurse's desk and take a seat for a moment to get some paperwork done.

"Jesus Darla, you look awful," Penelope says, and as I look up at her from my desk chair, I can feel warmth gathering in my face and settling in my cheeks and eye sockets.

"I'm just tired, it'll pass," I reply as I wave her off. Even though my head is beginning to pound, I take the clipboard in my hand and enter the information on my patient's sheet into the computer. *Another set of twins to begin adding to the maternity ward rounds... One's being sent off to the NICU...*

"Look a lot more than tired," Penelope says, her face ticked into a worried half-smile. "Let me take your temp."

"Penny, I don't got time for that." I sigh as I look at my watch, standing up quickly. Apparently it's far too fast because the next thing I remember is waking up in a hospital bed down in the emergency room. The headache I'd had from earlier was much worse as I lay there shivering under a stack of blankets.

"Ah, glad to see you're awake," Doctor Lee says, a troubled look on his face as he shuts off his flashlight. "I was starting to get worried there."

"What happened?" I ask with a groan.

"Well, you took a pretty nasty fall upstairs on the labor ward," Doctor Lee replies. "You gave Penny quite the scare."

"I'm fine," I insist, and I go to sit up. Immediately, I regret it, the pounding in my head roaring as pain shoots to my eyebrow. I put my hand to my forehead, realizing that there's a bandage there, and when I gently press it I let out a gentle hiss as it's tender to the touch.

"Actually, no, you're not," Doctor Lee says as he helps me lay back down. "You have the flu."

"You've got to be kidding," I whine as I heave a heavy sigh.

"It was bound to happen sooner or later with as rampant as it's been around here, Darla," Doctor Lee says with a shrug. "The bigger deal here is that I'm now also a bit worried about a concussion to be honest."

"Well, that would explain the tenderness," I reply, frowning. *Of course, I'd have to be the one to beef it on the ward like a fool,* I think to myself. *Now all the girls are going to be yucking it up about it later. Well, whoever can even make it in...* "But if I can just rest awhile, I think I'll be good to go back up there."

"Oh no, you are not going back on the ward," Doctor Lee replies.

"Really?" I ask, my heart hopping into my throat.

"Yes, really," Doctor Lee replied with a smile. "But don't worry, I already talked to Doctor Proctor; I told him what happened, and we've called Yennifer in from ICU to fill your spot."

"Wait, you're sending me home?" I ask.

"If you're worried about a hit to your attendance, trust me, you've got enough sick days."

Yeah... but not paid ones at the moment. A big emphasis on the 'not being paid for it' part.

"But—"

"No buts, Darla," Doctor Lee replies with a shake of his finger. "You've got to go home. You're contagious and have a head injury. We can't have you getting the pregnant women or babies sick, you know that."

If Doctor Proctor were right in front of me, I knew I might be able to weasel my way into staying with some acetaminophen and an ice pack. But not with Doctor Lee. It isn't that Doctor Proctor is a bad guy, but he lived to work and expected that from everyone else. He's very much a pick yourself up by your bootstraps, dust yourself off, and keep going type of man.

Doctor Lee, however, is his polar opposite when it comes to personality and care for the workers. If you were sick or hurt, he'd find a way to get you out of there the best he could. Whether it was by sending you home early, or sometimes, letting you sleep it off in the resting area we have for the doctors and nurses to use on break.

Normally, being sent home would be fine... but we are really depending on the extra money. Instantly, I am worried about Joseph getting frustrated, but he's a reasonable man, and I know that I'm projecting my own insecurities onto him.

"I'll have Tabby come along with your discharge papers," Doctor Lee says after giving me a good look over. "I suggest calling Joe and trying to get a ride... your pupil dilation is alright, but I'd rather be safe. I tried calling already, but I didn't get an answer."

"Alright," I say, finding it curious he didn't answer. But I just brushed it off.

"Penny left your purse on the tray there," Doctor Lee says as he goes to leave the room. "Feel better, Darla."

"Thanks, Doc," I reply, and he gives me a smile and a little wave before heading back out into the atrium, slipping my folder into the stack for 'discharges' before grabbing another clipboard from intake and speed walking off.

"Shoot," I say as I snatch my purse up off the table and begin fishing through it until I finally find my cell phone. "It's two in the morning," I mutter to myself as I scroll through my contacts, find Joe, and immediately dread hitting the call button, once again overcome with the worry that he will be upset—the threat of disappointment my daddy would have had carrying over into my adult life. *He's going to be so irritated... he's finally got a day off tomorrow...*

I sit and wait, listening to the trill of the phone as it rings, waiting on bated breath for him to answer. However, instead of being met by his rich, velvety voice, I'm met with his jovial voicemail message, and I quickly hang up.

Weird, I think to myself as I call again, only to get the same result. *Did he turn his ringer off?* I ask myself as I try again. Same thing. Voicemail. *I mean, he might have the day off, but he's the neurosurgeon on call... he's got to have the thing turned on.*

After Tabby comes in with Tylenol and my release forms, I slowly creep out into the hallway, my bag slung over my shoulder. I don't want Doctor Lee to see me leaving without Joseph, so I peer through the glass, waiting until he ducks into another room to make my escape.

I'm confident that even though my head is thumping like a drum that I'll be fine. My vision isn't double or blurred so I scurry out to the parking lot, and head home. A part of me is sure that Joseph is okay, but we are in our forties now—anything can happen, and it's really bothering me that he's still not picking up.

I spent the whole drive home trying not to panic, reminding myself he just had a physical, and they'd given him a clean bill of health. But my mind was being vicious to me, remembering how my daddy had gone, fast and without warning. So, as I pull into the driveway, all I can think of is whether or not he's alright.

I rush out of the car and toward our big, beautiful home—a ranch house in the hills—that we'd bought years and years ago, and I quickly scuttle inside. Immediately, I'm hit by the scent of candles—warm apple pie to be exact, a scent that I buy in bulk whenever I can, my favorite.

It reminds me of being back home on the ranch with my folks in Kansas. The White Dahlia, named after my granny, memories of my mama in the kitchen making apple crisp and crumble. But Joseph has never been much of a candle burner himself. So, what's he doing burning my stash?

"Honey?" I call out, and instead of an answer, I hear shuffling coming from the back hall leading to our room. "Honey, are you alright?" I ask, but still no answer, and my heart begins to pound as I get closer and closer to the doorway and hear muffled, almost urgent whispers.

"What in the world is going on?" The words spill out of my mouth as I bust open the door to our bedroom with a swift kick, and I feel like my whole body is on fire when I don't find Joseph alone. Instead, there's a young woman in lingerie, her derriere hanging out as she tries to climb out the window, my makeup clattering off the small dresser she's standing on. "Hold it right there," I snap, and the lace-clad lady of the night freezes in place at the sound of my voice.

"Darla, I can explain. . . "

"Explain what? You in bed with this hussy?" I yell, and Joseph's face goes from a pale peach to a bright red as she pulls herself out of the window, nearly slipping and falling to the floor as she struggles to get down, covering her heaving bosom with her arms.

"There's no need for all that!" he yells as the woman cowers by the window, trying to bend down and gather up her clothes.

"I-I'm sorry, I didn't know," she sputters nervously. "He told me that he was separated and getting a divorce."

"Oh, is that so?" I say as I cock one hip, all the fatigue and weariness completely dissipating as I cross my arms over my chest.

"Darla, I—"

"You what? What? Go on and try to make some sort of excuse now!" I holler, adrenaline blasting through my veins as his face falls. He looks down into his lap as his mistress hurried to get dressed.

"Don't you worry, Joseph, I'll give you exactly what you want," I say as my voice begins to crack, and my eyes sting with tears. "Now, you take your harlot, and get out of my house," I say as I pick up his jeans near my feet and throw them at him hard, right in his face, before I turn on my heel and walk away.

I can hear arguing between the two of them as they hurry to get dressed, and I walk out into the living room, putting my head in my hands. *Don't you dare show any emotion,* I beg my brain and body. *Wait to cry until they leave. Don't even give him the satisfaction of knowing that he's got to you. It's obvious he could give a lick about how you feel, bringing another woman into your bed. You hold your head high and make him think you don't give a crap. He certainly didn't.*

She walks out first, sheepishly mouthing sorry to me, pumps in hand as she sneaks out the door. A few minutes later, Joseph follows with a couple of small suitcases in his hands. He stops and looks at me and shakes his head.

"You know, none of this would have happened if you were ever home," he says, and immediately I feel rage creep through my veins. *I have been working my tail off for us. For our home. For our farm. To keep the lives we've been living sustainable. . . and he dares to say something like that to me after I find him with some twenty-year-old filled with ten pounds of silicone?*

I let out a guttural scream before picking up the vase on the coffee table and chucking it at him.

"Get out!" I scream as I finally break, tears streaming down my face as the vase shatters against the wall, missing him by inches.

"Are you crazy?" Joseph yells, and I feel a little smirk creep into the side of my mouth as I hear Patsy Cline play in my mind.

And I'm crazy for loving you. . .

"Don't you ever come back here."

Chapter One

DARLA

I feel a wave of sadness wash over me as I begin to wrap up all my little cow collectibles in old newspapers that Sparrow brought me, gently placing them into a box heavily cushioned by bubble wrap. The more I pack, the more the old house gets emptier and emptier, and while I hate leaving it all behind, I know that I can't afford it anymore.

I'd won the house in the rather messy divorce, able to prove he was adulterous quite easily, so to lose it here now feels like such a big loss. Maybe that sounds a bit petty, but when your heart's been ripped in two by the man you stood by for nearly thirty years, it had felt good to keep it. The farm had always been my passion project anyways. But on my income, I just couldn't swing it, and I was going more and more into debt.

Sadly, the slow descent into debt meant that one by one, all my beloved animals had to be sold to try to keep the house afloat. I'd tried my best to keep them, but it just wasn't working no matter what I did. The last of them to go, Laney, nearly broke my heart all over again. I'd raised her from a foal, and she felt like one of my children. I kept her as long as I could. I'd even tried to find a smaller house with at least a tiny horse barn and some land. But, in the end, I couldn't afford anything that had what Laney would truly need to be happy. And you know what they say. . . if you truly love something, let it go. So, I did just that, and it still stings.

After selling the animals, I thought that maybe if I could get ahead, I could keep up with everything, but I just couldn't. Not alone. My friends suggested asking the kids for help, but I wasn't about to disrupt little Joe's or Sparrow's life with my drama. They had their own lives. So, I sold the house, telling them all that I did it because I needed a fresh start, and honestly, I think I do.

I mean, after what I'd discovered happening in my own bed, it's probably for the best. I couldn't bear to go in there, let alone sleep in the room I'd shared for decades with Joseph. Even after Sparrow, my daughter, helped me get a new bed... I still couldn't sleep in that room... and I began to hate living in a house full of heartbreak. The living room became my new bedroom, not wanting to disturb either of the kids' old rooms in case they were to ever need it.

So, I sold the house, and decided to move south to Thistleberry.

"You doin' okay, Mama?" Sparrow asks as she comes up behind me with Jade, my first grandbaby, who smiles at me with a droopy grin.

"Yes, just a lot of tedious work here," I replied. "I didn't realize how many little knickknacks and trinkets I really had 'til I started packing everything up."

"To be fair, we did buy you the cows all the time," Sparrow pointed out as she picked up the very first cow figure I'd got as a wedding present—two cute little cows in wedding gear—and I try my best to blink back tears.

It seems so surreal that Joseph had done what he did, and that we wouldn't be spending the rest of our lives together like we'd always talked about. We had been together since we were sixteen, married almost thirty years, and I'm still unsure of why he did what he did.

There had been no signs that he was straying away from me. I mean, we had both been working a ton... little did I know that it had more to do with him courting other girls than it had been about the bills going up. It was a hard pill to swallow. I had thought that we were the perfect team, like Dolly Parton and Carl Dean. But I had been wrong, and it still hurts. Like a festering, open wound that time isn't seeming to heal.

I guess that old saying is wrong.

"Why don't you keep that one, darlin'," I say to her as she gives me a curious look. "I know you like it, and I already have so many."

"Oh, okay, thanks," she says as she wraps it, puts it in newspaper, and places it in the bib pocket of her shortalls before placing little Jade on the floor to roll around. "So, you excited about moving down to Thistleberry?"

CHAPTER ONE

From what I can tell, Thistleberry seems like a nice little town. It's much smaller than what I'm used to here in Amarillo, but I suppose I really don't need much. It's not like I go out and galivant around the city anyways. All I need is a nice, cozy little place to lay my head, close to Sparrow, her husband, Daniel, and my grandbaby, Jade.

I'm a bit sad that Joe wants to stay in Amarillo, but he's a grown man, and there's not much I can do about that. He says he'll visit, but his visits are so sparse even now that I doubt he will live up to that promise. He's a busy man, working some highfalutin office job, and I'm proud of him.

But I can't worry about all that. I have to do what's right for me. Even if this whole situation sucks.

"To be honest, it's a bit weird you know?" I say with a sigh. "I've been here so long. I'm used to my job here, and my friends. . . though I'm glad you'll be close."

"I get it, it's a lot to have happened in a year," Sparrow says. "I felt homesick for a long while when I moved away."

My little Sparrow, always the good girl. Always trying to figure out how to help someone or heal an ailing heart.

"Well, I suppose that's just how it is huh?" I say as I wrap up another cow figurine and place it gently inside the box, forcing a smile.

"You know, if you're worried about not knowing anyone, you could use this one app that my friends use," Sparrow replies.

"Oh yeah?"

"Mm-hmm! It, uh, helps you make friends at the very least," Sparrow says. But I can tell by the inflection in her voice, and the impish grin on her face, that she's scheming something.

She gets that from her daddy.

"What kind of an app is it?" I ask, interested in what mischievous thing she has up her sleeve.

"It's called Love and Company," she says a bit quietly, and I let out a chuckle.

"Now that doesn't seem like an app for just friends, little bird," I reply, shaking my head.

"Well, it's for both, you know?" Sparrow says. "Finding friends. . . maybe kick up a little romance."

"Now, I know you mean well, but I'm not at all ready to go out looking for someone new," I say as I begin chuckling nervously. "I don't need that headache."

"Oh, don't be like that," Sparrow replies, rolling her eyes.

"It's true," I say with a shrug. "Why would I want to trade one headache for another?"

"Not everyone is a jerk like Dad, Mama," Sparrow insists.

"Yeah, and look where chasing tail got your father, hmm?" I say, and Sparrow can't help but burst into laughter.

"Like you always say, karma comes for those who deserve it," Sparrow replies with a shrug.

"That's not funny," I scold her, but really, it is. Destiny had some crazy plans for Joseph, that was for sure, and it was all due to his little girlfriend. . . who also turned out to be a professional con artist.

Ms. thing was wanted in several states for the extortion of a handful of older men, blackmailing them into giving her their money—though I don't know the details as to what exactly she had on them. Not only that, but apparently she'd hurt a few of them, and they were looking for her all over. . . and found out that she was with Joseph.

Since ol' Joe didn't fit the elderly, rich profile of men she'd usually take advantage of, the police assumed he was in on it too, and before I knew it, the Amarillo police department had been at my door asking if I knew where he was. But he had high tailed it out of Texas from what little Joe had said and was on the lam. A bit of just deserts if I don't say so myself.

God does work in mysterious ways after all.

"Come on, it won't hurt to give it a try," Sparrow says, and she reaches down on the couch, picks up my phone, and begins messing around with it. Her thumbs and fingers quickly tap all over the screen before she hands it over to me.

"There," she says. "Now you have it, and you can check it out when you want to."

"Thank you," I say as I heave a sigh and shove the phone in my pocket. We continue packing together, taking breaks for Sparrow to feed little Jade and for us to play with her.

We take a break to eat dinner, and then once it's dark, they turn into bed in Sparrow's old bedroom, leaving me to myself in the living room where I continue to wrap each figure carefully, unable to settle down.

Once I'm alone, I pull my phone out to check the weather and right on the front page of my phone is that app. Its stylish, little pink logo beckons me to take a look as my finger hovers over it.

Not a chance, I think to myself as I click on the weather app and settle down on the couch. Once I get there, I'll make friends at work, I'm sure. I don't need some sort of magic app to help me with that, and I certainly don't need to try to find someone new. Why would I want to waste the next thirty years with someone just to end up alone and disappointed all over again?

 I don't think my heart could take it.

Chapter Two

Eli

A gentle breeze wafts into the window, and I open my eyes before my alarm goes off, the world outside still pitch black even as the

suncatcher on the porch begins to chime. It's a nonsensical melody that is somehow still easy on the ears. I smile as I lay there for a

moment, remembering when my sweet Melanie had hung it up when we'd first moved in, telling me we needed a little color and flair

in our stark white farmhouse.

After a while, I stretch my arms and legs, roll over to get out of bed, glance at her picture on the nightstand, and heave a little sigh.

"Mornin' Mel," I say like I do every day before I get up and go to my dresser, hop out of my pj's, and get dressed for the day. But

today, I'm trying to look more professional than usual. I've got a potential new hire coming in, and I want to look the part of a boss—

not just some scruffy rancher.

But first, it's time to make breakfast.

I turn on the small radio on the shelf, and as "Chattahoochee" starts to play, I put on Mel's old apron and begin to make breakfast for the boys and I. I make us cheesy scrambled eggs, toast, and some bacon, and then pour each one of us a cool glass of milk.

It may be just after the holidays, but in Texas it's still hot, and already that heat is trying to eek in through the window over the sink I

got open to stop the bacon I'm cooking from smoking up the house.

"Well, hello there," I say as Noah lumbers in, still half asleep.

"Morning Dad," he replies as he plops down in his spot, and I slide his plate in front of him. He's never been much of a morning

person.

"Mornin'," I reply. "You look like you had a rough night."

"My ac stopped working in the middle of the night," he replies with a yawn.

"Ugh," I say, making a face. "I'll take a look after we get the animals fed."

"Well, look at you, looking all spiffy," Zack says as he strolls into the room, the yin to Noah's yang, chipper as ever, like a ray of sunshine

in the morning. Though I suppose that makes sense, it seems twins are usually that way. At least my two are anyways.

"He's even pulled out the ol' bolo tie," Noah teases as he picks up a piece of bacon and chomps down on it.

"I got an interview at nine," I reply as I hand Zack his plate and then sit down at the head of the table, my eyes drifting off to Melanie's

old spot as the two boys talk amongst themselves. Sometimes, I swear I can still smell her perfume in the air. . .

"You alright, Dad?" Zack asks.

"Y-yeah," I reply, snapping out of my memories of Melanie and I dancing in the kitchen and back to reality. "Just tired, I guess."

"Well, don't let your food get cold now," Noah teases as he shovels a fork full of eggs into his mouth.

"About that interview," Zack says.

"What about it?" I ask.

"Do you really need to interview someone just to muck stalls?" Zack asks. "It's not like it's rocket science or anything."

"He's got a point," Noah chimes in, "it's just basic chorin'."

"Well, I don't see either of you two volunteering to do it," I reply as I take a bite of toast with raspberry jam. "It's getting harder and harder to get some of you to do your chores even," I say as my eyes drift over to Noah, and Zack grins.

"Come on, Pop, cut me some slack," Noah groans. "I just want to get to know Becky better."

"Courtin' Becky can come after chorin'," I say with a chuckle, and Zack stifles a laugh as we all chat amongst ourselves, shooting the

breeze while we enjoy the rest of our breakfast. There's only one thing missing that could make the morning better. But she's been

missing a long time now. And even though that's been my reality for so long, every day I wake up and she isn't there is still as jarring

as the last.

"Alright, now just because I'm doing an interview doesn't mean you two get to dilly dally," I say as I get my fancy jacket on. "I'm going

to head up to the office and do some paperwork I'm behind on while I wait for this guy. But you two need to get to feedin' and

muckin'"

"Yeah, we got it," Noah sighs as he finishes his plate, washing it quickly and putting it in the drainer to air dry. "Good luck with the new hire."

"Thanks," I say as I head out, hop into my beat-up ol' truck, and head toward the office, which is toward the front gates of the massive

property I own. Not to toot my own horn, but out of all the ranches in the area, my grass is the greenest, and my animals seem the

happiest, which is something I take massive pride in.

Not everyone seems to have the same dedication that me and the boys do, but that seems to be how it is these days. Working hard

has dwindled down to hardly workin', and as I walk into the office to work on some quarterly tax papers, I wonder if this guy coming in

is going to be another dud. I've had plenty of ranch hands come and go, and some of them were great. But the last one—

unbeknownst to the kids—had been a felon, and he'd tried to rob my accounts dry, which is why the interview is important to me.

While I believe that everyone deserves a second chance, I can't risk it again on my land. It probably sounds a bit prejudiced, but if someone looks like trouble, I'm not about to hire them on. This ranch is my life's work. My blood, sweat, and tears are in its soil, and I won't let anyone mess with what I've built. No way, no how.

"Excuse me, I take it this is the office." I hear a man say.

"Oh jeez, I didn't even hear you knock," I say as I look up to see a man a little younger than me wearing a black cowboy hat, a black

dress shirt, and Wrangler jeans. He's a bit scruffy, but I don't mind so much. Being a bit scruffy doesn't mean you're bad news.

"It's alright," he says with a smile, his teeth almost blindingly pearly white, which is a good sign, I suppose. Means he takes care of

himself, despite not shaving. "I'm Mitch," he says as he steps into the office, leans forward, and juts his hand out toward me.

"Nice to meet you Mitch, I'm Eli, the owner of the ranch," I say, and his eyes widen a bit.

"Oh wow, wasn't expecting the owner to be giving the interview," Mitch replies.

"Yeah, well, we are a family business," I say as I motion for him to sit down in the seat in front of my desk. "So, Mitch, I guess my first

question is how long have you been working ranch jobs?"

"As long as I can remember," he replies. "My daddy was a farrier, and we had our own ranch growing up."

"Oh really? Where?" I ask.

"Amarillo," he replies.

"Oh really? I got a cousin living over in Amarillo."

"Yeah, it's pretty nice, but I'm originally from Kansas," Mitch says with a smile. "We moved to Texas when I was five or so."

"Some good ranches over in Kansas," I say.

"My uncle runs River Rose," Mitch replies.

"Oh wow, that's in Topeka, right?"

"Westmoreland, actually."

"Well, that's not too far away from Topeka, is it?"

"About an hour or so," Mitch replies. "But going there was a treat. And once we moved here, we moved out to the sticks, and Dad

started up our own ranch."

"Oh, wow! So, you've always been on a farm," I say.

"Basically," Mitch agrees. "A lot of my friends hated being in the country, but I didn't mind it one bit. On the ranch, we had most things we needed, and the general stores and supply places in town had the rest."

"Makes sense," I say with a smile. "So, you worked for your daddy about how long in total?"

"Until last year," Mitch says, but his upbeat tone shifts a bit, and I can tell by the look in his eyes that something is up.

"Why did you end up leavin'?" I ask, not wanting to leave the stone unturned and regret it later.

"I left after my wife died, actually," Mitch says, and I can see the flicker of pain in his eyes. Immediately, I feel terrible for even asking.

"Oh!" I say, shocked. I wasn't expecting that. "I'm so sorry, I didn't mean to bring that up."

"It's okay, it's not like you could've known," Mitch replies. "She fought a hard battle with leukemia. We moved down here to be closer to the better hospitals, but it wasn't enough."

I feel all my muscles tighten as a wave of sadness washes over me. *This poor guy,* I think to myself as I watch him struggle to keep his composure. It's all too visceral, a reminder of how I was when I first lost Melanie. Even ten years later, it still stings like the dickens.

"Can I be honest with you?" Mitch asks.

"Of course," I reply.

"I don't know how many other applicants you have, and I don't want to seem like some groveling sissy, but I really need this job," Mitch says. "There are medical bills, funeral bills, the mortgage on the new place. . . I thought I could hack it alone out here, but it's all piling up on me now."

"I can imagine," I reply with a frown. "Say, since you know so much about ranching, would you want to come on full-time instead?" I ask.

"Really?" Mitch asks, seemingly shocked.

"Well sure," I said, trying to not make it seem like I was throwing him a pity bone, not wanting to step on his toes. "I could use a man with your expertise and experience, and it pays a lot more than just mucking."

"Well, shoot! Yeah, I'll take the job," Mitch says as he juts his hand out and we shake on it.

"When can you start?" I asked.

"Well, gosh, I guess as soon as you need me," Mitch replies, beaming big and bright, the look on his face bringing a bit of warmth to

my soul. I know in a way what he's going through, and something is compelling me to help him. I mean, it felt like it was the right

thing to do after all. Can't just let a man who just lost his wife suffer. . . though the subject itself hits a bit closer to home than I'd like.

It's almost time. . . the tenth anniversary of when my wife had been taken from us keeps getting closer, and I feel like maybe if I can ease his pain, I can quell my own. . . if only a little bit.

Chapter Three

DARLA

"Finally! That's the last one," I say with a grunt as I set the box labeled 'plates' on the kitchen counter, wiping a bead of sweat from my brow.

"Hard to believe that the whole farmhouse can fit in here," Sparrow says.

"Are you making fun of my new house?" I tease, raising my eyebrow at her.

"No! I love it; it's so cozy," Sparrow insists.

"You mean tiny?" I ask, raising an eyebrow.

"C'mon now, don't put words in my mouth." Sparrow frowns and I can't help but laugh.

"Well, it's just me now since you and little Joe are adults, you know?" I reply as I lean against the counter. "But I do have the one guest room if it's ever needed."

"It's definitely gorgeous in here," Sparrow remarks as she runs her fingertips against the lacquered cherrywood wall.

"Well of course it is, your mama has good taste," I say with a wink. "Thank you two for taking the time to help me move."

"It's really no problem, Mrs. M," Daniel, Sparrow's husband, says with a smile as Jade babbles in her little play chair. "Just glad we could help."

"Well, I appreciate it all the same," I reply. "I'm hungry, why don't I treat us all to Chinese?"

"Ooh! That would be awesome!" Sparrow chimes in cheerfully, Chinese being one of her favorite foods. "Can we get some sesame chicken?"

"Of course! I'll grab some of that, lo mein, some fried rice, beef and broccoli. . . and what was that one thing you like Danny?"

"Oh, um, shrimp and scallops in the spicy garlic sauce," Daniel replies. "You got it!" I pick up my cell phone and look up the local

Chinese place and put in our order. It's not long before they get to the house, and all of us begin to chow down, sitting crisscross on

the hardwood floor, famished from unloading the truck since early on in the morning without any of us except Sparrow taking a break

to feed Jade.

"So, when do you start at the new hospital?" Sparrow asks.

"Monday," I reply, and it's obvious that Sparrow isn't thrilled about it, her eyebrows furrowed.

"Are you serious?" she gasps.

"Well yeah, Bird, what's the point in waiting?" I ask.

"You just did a big move across Texas," Sparrow replies. "It's a bit crazy that you're not going to take any time to settle in and unpack,

or get used to the town, Mama."

"I don't really have a choice, honey, I need to be able to pay the bills," I reply.

"You worry me," Sparrow replies as Jade begins to whine, and she picks her up out of her play chair to let her roll around on the floor.

"You could have asked Daniel and I to cover your first month of the mortgage, you know."

"Yeah, definitely," Daniel agrees. Daniel makes quite a bit of money as the CEO of his own tech company, and as much as it would

make things convenient to hop on his offer, I'd feel weird doing it. A mom takes care of her kids, not the other way around.

"I appreciate the thought, but it's really no big deal," I reply. "Besides, I'll have all weekend to settle in."

I don't want to worry, Sparrow, but to be honest, I was lucky to get the house that I got. Joseph had apparently made some not-too-great decisions I wasn't aware of, in my name—probably due to that little jezebel he'd messed around with. So, my credit wasn't the best. Plus, even with the house being smaller, and the mortgage being less, it was still expensive to handle all on my own.

"If you say so," Sparrow replies as I look in the bag, searching for the sugar buns I'd ordered with our food, but unfortunately, they aren't there.

"Oh no, they forgot our dessert!" I groan, sporting a frown.

"Mom, it's totally fine, don't worry about it," Sparrow replies as she helps Jade eat some noodles.

"Yeah, it's really not that big of a deal," Daniel agrees. "It's not like we'll die without them."

"Nonsense, you guys deserve it after today," I say as I throw my paper plate in the garbage. "Let me go run to the store really quick and knab us a pie."

I get up, run to the bedroom, and find my suitcase full of my usual clothes and work stuff, changing out of my dusty moving clothes and into one of my favorite dresses. I go into the bathroom, pin up my hair a bit, and slap on some ruby red lipstick before I grab my purse from the kitchen and head to the door, slipping my heels on. "I'll be right back," I say, only to be surprised as I reach for knob that there's a knock on the door.

"Ooh, maybe that's the delivery guy," I say to myself as I open the door. "Hi, thanks for coming back—"

I stop mid-sentence, my smile completely disintegrating as my jaw slacks, and I look up at the tall person in front of me. It isn't the charming, Chinese delivery guy from earlier that I'd flirted a little with. No, it's someone I thought I'd never have to lay eyes on again nor had I wanted to.

"Hey, Darla," Joseph says. "Nice to see you."

"Can't say I can say the same," I reply as I cross my arms against my chest and lean against the door frame, glaring at him. "What are you doing here?"

"Now that's no way to act, Darla," Joseph replies. "I come in peace."

"Sure, you do," I reply. "And I'm the pope."

"I came here to talk," Joseph says as he seems to ignore my sarcasm entirely.

"About what?" I ask.

"Us," Joseph says as a smile spreads across his face. "The future."

"Come again?" I ask, hit with a wave of surprise at first, which rapidly changes to an unimpressed leer.

"I just think that maybe we may have been a bit too hasty with all this divorce stuff," he replies, and his answer boils my blood. I lost my animals, my horse, and my home. I constantly felt inadequate, even when I dressed to the nines in my old pin-up outfits to try to drag myself out of my depression... and now this sad sack wants to make amends after a year? After he signed the divorce papers because he thought that hot little twenty-whatever was his new love? Outrageous.

"I don't think so," I reply dryly, and Joseph's face twists into one of shock.

"You can't be serious," Joseph replies.

"Dead serious," I reply. "The time for talking about us went out the window the moment I found you in our bed with—what was her name? Lilith?" I say, arching my eyebrow. "She is quite the she-devil, huh?"

"Ha ha, very funny," Joseph replies. "I don't care about her, sugar. I never loved her like I do you."

"Ah, yes, because you definitely cheat on the person you love," I say, rolling my eyes. "Get real, Joe."

"I'm serious. What you and I had was special—"

"Special enough to throw it all away to chase tail?" I ask. "You have a lot of nerve showing up here trying to mess with my emotions like this."

"I promise it's not like that," Joseph insists. "I get that I messed up, babe... but life is so short, Darla. There's always room for second chances."

"Not with us there isn't," I reply. "You may have stolen nearly thirty years of my life from me, but I will be keeping my dignity intact, thanks."

Joseph's face turns from friendly to frustrated, the muscles of his jaw clenching a bit as he struggled not to show that he was getting angry. But once you've been with someone for so long, it's easy to pick up on stuff like that.

"You won't even hear me out?" Joseph asks.

"How did you even find me?" I ask, totally ignoring his question. We'd lived out in the countryside in Amarillo, and our closest

neighbor had been miles away. So, it couldn't have been them. The only other people it could have been was my coworkers at the

hospital, but there was no way any of the girls on the labor and delivery ward would have talked. They all hated him. Plain and simple.

And honestly? I feel much the same way.

"Wasn't too hard. I stopped by the post office and said that I was trying to get ahold of you, and Brett gave me your forwarding

address," Joseph said with a shrug.

"Well, you can tell Brett that he can kiss his job goodbye because I have half a mind to call his supervisor!"

"Mama, is everything okay out here?" Sparrow asks as she steps outside. Her eyes lock on Joseph and her demeanor immediately

sours. "What are you doing here?"

"Nice to see you too, Sparrow," Joseph says. "I'm here to talk to your mother."

"Well then, you'll be talking to my taillights because I'm going to the store," I say as I stomp off toward my car.

"Come on, don't be like that," Joseph begs. "Just come inside, we can talk about it all."

"There's nothing to discuss Joe," I assert as I go to open my car door. However, as I reach for the handle, he leans against the car,

trying to get in the way.

"Just let me stay Darla, please," Joseph pleads, and I can see the desperation in his eyes.

"I don't want nothing to do with harboring a fugitive," I say as I open the door and glare right into his eyes. "I'm not about to be your

stepping stone, Joe."

"Darla!" he cries out as I shut my door. I roll the window down, and he smiles, probably expecting me to give in. But instead, I give him

a smirk back.

"Good luck to you, Joe," I say. "You better be off my property by the time I get back."

"You don't mean that," Joseph says as he rushes to the other side, and I lock the door.

"I do," I reply. "I mean it with every fiber of my being."

"You're going to regret this," Joseph says as he jiggles the handle, his face becoming redder and redder by the second.

"You know," I say as I smile, even though it's killing me inside to watch him flounder. "I don't think I will," I say as I start the car and

crank up the radio as I begin to back out of the driveway while he continues to follow on foot.

Tears threaten to stream down my cheeks as it hits me—even though I am so angry at him, that I feel so much hatred and resentment

toward him. . . a part of me still cares deep down. Still wants to be there for him. But I can't and won't let that side win out. I will never

ever let anyone treat me like Joe did. Not ever again. Not even if I still love them. That sweet innocent, summer child Darla is gone, and

I won't let him think for a second that he can ever get me back.

I rev the engine, hit the gas, and peel out of that driveway, leaving him in the rearview, coughing on my dust. As I speed down the

road toward town, I choke down my tears so I don't make a mess of my makeup. I don't want to look like an unhinged ragamuffin on

my first trip to the store.

First appearances are everything, you know.

Chapter Four

Eli

It's been a long day of feeding, mucking, and ranching, and my dogs are barking as I head into the shed and look for the feed for my

oldest horse, Tango. He's an old dapple gray, the very first horse we ever got when we moved to the ranch, in fact, and he's pushing on

in years. About twenty-five I reckon, and he needs special feed and such, unlike the newer, younger horses. Easier stuff to chew with

more vitamins and such to help with bone health.

"Shoot," I sigh to myself as I sift through the bags of feed.

"What's wrong?" Mitch asks, coming up behind me with a mucking rake in his hand, setting it against the wall next to some other

tools.

"We're out of that senior horse feed for Tango," I reply as I get up with a grunt, my knees starting to weaken, not what they once were.

Guess I'll need some of that feed soon too, I think to myself, holding back a chuckle. Fifty-four isn't some spring chicken.

"Aw shoot," Mitch replies. "Did you want me to go get it?" he asks, and I look at my wristwatch and shake my head.

"Nah, it's nearly six now. You've already stayed way longer than you should have for the day," I say as I walk out of the shed and into

the sun, its rays warming my face. "Just make sure all the tools you've been using are put away and head home."

"Well, alright then," Mitch replies as he follows me out. "I'll see you tomorrow then."

"Yep, I'll catch ya later," I say as I pat my back pocket to make sure my wallet was still there and head for my truck. I crank up the tunes

and head out to town, tapping my fingers on the steering wheel to Clint Black's "Like the Rain" as I weave through the hills.

I make it to town just as the radio's DJ switches for the night crew, signaling that it was finally six. The six o' clock crew played mostly

new stuff, and while I don't hate the newer stuff, I'm definitely a nineties and older kind of country man.

Give me Travis Tritt, Clint Black, Joe Diffie, Mark Chestnut... even Shania if you had me in the right mood. Mel had loved her, that's for

sure. Her and those Dixie Chicks, but I suppose they're not called that anymore. The Chicks is what they're called now, I think. Either

way, the nineties were an amazing time for me, a time when love had found me. I cherish them and those songs deeply. They remind

me of better times.

I stepped into a supply store and, much to my frustration, had to try two others before I found Tango's feed, everyone else but

Weatherby's out of stock. As I lifted the two bags I'd snagged and put them into the back of my old Ford F-350, I felt my pocket

vibrate. I dipped my hand in and pulled out my phone, unlocked the screen, and saw that Zack had texted.

Hey Dad, since you're downtown, do you think you could stop at the store and grab me some deodorant and some snacks? Honey

mustard pretzels, pickles, and some salt and vinegar chips?

Sure, I replied as I climbed into the cabin of the truck and chuckled to myself. *You're going to become a pickle at this rate with all those*

pickles and salt.

Luckily, when I pull into the parking lot of the store, it's pretty dead, which is probably not so great for the store but great for me. I'm not really much of a man for crowds, nor do I really socialize much, so I avoid them any time I can. Plus, it means I can actually get to

the butcher counter to talk to Alan about bringing a few cows down for him to take care of and sell. Something I've been meaning to

do for weeks.

I grab a handbasket and get to work, first grabbing a few things I knew we would need soon, remembering that we were out of bacon,

having used the rest on breakfast this morning. Then, I began to start on Zack's little list.

Admittedly, I'm distracted by my own thoughts as I quickly glance down at my phone screen when suddenly, something slams me

square in the chest as I turn down the chip isle, something hard. When I look away from my phone and down at my chest, it's covered

in bits of blueish-purple goop and crusty flakes, alongside a couple of soft blueberries. The aroma of pie fills my nose.

"Ow!" I hear a whine drift up from the floor, and my eyes glance from my light blue button-up and down toward the sound to see a

rather beautiful woman sitting there on the tile floor. She's about my age, no, younger, I think. . . equally covered in pie, and the rest of

it is crumbled all around her in clumps. Immediately, I feel terrible. Her tight-fitting, red and white dress no doubt completely ruined

by the mess I'd caused.

She must be new, I think to myself as I realize I've never seen her face before. *No one dresses like that around here. Even her hair*

reminds of the old pin-up mags my grandpa used to have in the garage, pin curls and all. Almost too Hollywood to ever be from Texas.

She's. . . gorgeous.

"Ms., I am so sorry," I say as I put out my hand to try to help her up. "I can give you the money for a new dress or some dry cleaning or

something." But her piercing brown eyes leer at me from beneath her doe-like lashes with an icy stare as she smacks my hand away from her, her eyes glazed over with tears.

"What is wrong with you?" she exclaims, pushing herself up to her feet and pulling off her leather gloves, doing her best to brush what

she could off the front of her—anything that wasn't stuck to the fabric of her dress.

CHAPTER FOUR

The southern twang in her voice revealed that she was, at the very least, from the south. But her attitude was certainly not the good

old calm, cool, and collected tone I'd come to know in my fifty-four years. In fact, it caught me off guard.

"Don't you know how to look where you're going?" she asks, her voice seeming to become more and more angry by the second.

"I said I was sorry," I reply, and she shakes her head.

"That's what you men always think solves it, huh? Sorry, as if that ever means a dang thing," she spits and I'm taken aback by one, her

sudden affront to all men just from an accident and two, her entire demeanor in general.

Maybe she's having a bad day, I think to myself as I try to figure out a way to diffuse the situation. "Listen, Ms., I don't want any trouble

here, I promise. I'm just trying to do the right thing."

She begins to sob, shaking her head. "The only right thing you could have done was watch what you were doing, you. . . you. . . lunkhead!"

"Lunkhead?" I repeat, flabbergasted at her escalation. "Lady, it was an accident, it's not the end of the world."

"Oh, can it!" she says. "If you hadn't been eyes deep into your phone, looking at God knows what, this wouldn't have happened."

"I was looking at my son's list of things he needed," I reply, my voice raising as I can feel the prickles of anger begin to burn in my

arms. "As if you never made a mistake in your life."

Suddenly, her face goes from angry to upset, and she begins to sob, like she's a living mood swing. "Screw you!" she manages to

choke out, and before I can get another word in edgewise, she's already stomping toward the front door, her pumps clicking loudly

with every step.

"Jeezum crow," I hear a voice say behind me, "that was intense."

"What a nut job," I say as a teenage boy from the checkout comes over and hands me some paper towels to wipe off my shirt.

"Thanks."

"No problem," the kid says. "Sorry about that, I'll have to call Glen to come clean this up."

"You don't got to bother the janitor," I said as I finished cleaning myself up and got on my hands and knees. "I got this if you've got

some cleaner at your register. Was my fault anyways."

The helpful clerk scurried off and came back with a bottle of spray cleaner and a little trash bag, and I went to work, cleaning up the

obliterated blueberry pie from the floor. After I got it all up, I picked my basket back up and went right back to shopping, though I

tried to cautiously rush through it.

I skipped talking to Alan, not too keen on spending much more time in the store with pie all over me, and made it back to the register,

only to be checked out by the nice young man who had helped me earlier.

"Gosh, what a weird woman, huh?" he says.

"Yeah, well, you don't know what someone's going through I suppose," I say as he rings up my groceries. I pull out my wallet, pay in

cash, leave him a tip while he's distracted—so he can't argue with me about it—and head back out to the truck.

I carefully peel off the shirt and fold the mess in on itself so none of it gets on my seat, leaving me in my black undershirt and jeans.

Welp, I'm going to definitely need another shower, I think to myself as I take a closer look in the rearview, noticing there's blueberry

streaked across my face, my ear, and even in my hair.

By the time I get back home, it's getting late, nearly seven-thirty. When I get through the door, Zack and Noah are sitting at the table,

waiting patiently like two pups at supper time.

"Hey!" Noah calls out, nose in his phone.

"Evening," I reply as I push the door open with my foot, hands full of grocery bags as I hand Zack his.

"Where's my snacks?" Noah whines as he gives me a weird look.

"You didn't text," I say with a shrug.

"What happened to your shirt? Is that the new fashion now? To go out in a tank top?" Zack teased. "Wait a minute, what's on your face?"

"It's a long story," I reply as I put on Mel's apron and grab the bag of chicken I'd marinated from the fridge and put it on the counter.

"Well, it's been a boring day, and we got time," Noah replies.

"I was at the store, and some crazy lady ran into me with her pie," I reply.

"Oof," Noah replies as I grab the shirt I'd brought in to soak and show them the damage.

"Golly! She really did slam into you," Zack says.

"Actually, it was my fault," I say, correcting myself. "I was looking down at my phone and whacked into her. Ruined her dress and everything."

"Hmm, it's almost like someone shouldn't be paying attention so closely to their phone," Zack teased, echoing a statement that I find myself saying to the boys daily.

"Well, I could have just not got your stuff then, huh?" I sassed back as Noah burst into laughter.

"Ah, good point," Zack says with a nod.

"You said she was crazy though? How do you know that?" Noah asks.

"Well, usually when someone makes a mistake, they don't scream like a dang banshee over it," I say with a sigh as I pull the meat out of the bag, slap it onto the cutting board, and begin tenderizing it a bit with the meat mallet.

"She yelled at you?" Zack asks.

"Yep, made a complete scene out of the whole ordeal," I reply in between whacks. "I even offered to pay for her dress or dry cleaning, but she was going off about how men never mean nothing they say or some garbage."

"Sounds like someone was already in their feelings," Zack replies.

"You're probably right," I agree. "Don't matter though. You can't—"

"Take your feelings out on others," the boys say, completing my thought.

"Exactly," I say with a smile as I pull a pan out from the cupboard, lay the chicken breasts in the pan, and then slide them in the oven before starting a timer.

"Well, hopefully she finds peace," Zack says.

"Yeah, well, as long as it's far away from me, that'll be just fine," I say as the three of us crack up. "Now. is someone going to help me peel these potatoes?"

"I'll do it," Zack says as he gets up, grabs the bag of potatoes, and starts washing some in the sink before bringing them to the table to peel. My eyes look toward the calendar. Only one more day before that dreaded day. . . and even though it's been ten years, I still just want to hole up in my room and sit there and ignore the world.

But I know I can't.

I've got to keep moving, even if it hurts.

Chapter Five

Darla

"I'm back!" I call out as jovially as I can muster as I kick off my shoes, the sun starting to set behind the hills. It's taken me twice the

time to get the pie for dessert, having driven all the way out to San Antonio after embarrassing myself at the grocery store in town.

Everyone gawked at me in both places and not because I was some beautiful bombshell. But because I looked like a hot mess. Which,

to be fair, at the moment, isn't far from the truth.

So much for first impressions.

"Oh my gosh, Ma," Sparrow gasps. "What happened to your dress?"

"You know, I don't think I want to talk about it," I say as I hand Sparrow the pie and a half gallon of French vanilla ice cream, and then

walk into the bedroom and quickly slip into something more comfortable. . . and less covered in pie.

"Joseph take off after I left?" I ask as I walk back out to the living room.

"Took a bit of convincing from Daniel, but he left," Sparrow says.

"I hope he wasn't too much trouble," I reply, feeling bad for leaving them there with Joseph. Not that I thought that Joseph would hurt anybody, but because of the tension between them all since Joseph had done what he did.

"It was really no trouble," Daniel insisted.

"Well, let's get that pie in the oven and warm it up," I say as I force a smile. "I hope y'all love some apple crumble."

"Sounds good to me," Sparrow says as we preheat the oven. "I'm sorry about Dad," Sparrow apologizes.

"It's not your fault darlin'," I insist. "He's acting like a hit dog, even though he's the one that caused all of this."

"Well, I'm sorry all the same," Sparrow says as she wraps her arms around me, squeezing me tight.

"Thank you," I say as I hold back tears. When the pie was ready, I cut it up as we chatted about anything other than Joseph or what

happened at the store. "Aw, you guys," I gasp and smile as we all sit around the dining room table that they'd put back together while

I was gone. "It looks good!" "We figured it would be better than sitting on the floor," Daniel said. "Plus, I found the electric drill in the

box labeled 'tools'." "It came out really well," I say as I hand out slices of pie with paper plates and forks. "Anyone want ice cream?"

"Yes please!" both Sparrow and Daniel say, and we all giggle as we eat our warm apple pie. The pie reminds me of my own mother, of

Amarillo. . . of the life I'd shared with Joseph only for him to wreck it all. . . and I can't hold it in anymore.

"Sorry," I say quietly as I leave my pie and retreat to my bedroom, closing the door behind me as I sit down hard on the bed. I begin to sob, my head in my hands, when Sparrow swoops in.

"Oh, Mama," Sparrow says as she sits down next to me, gives me a side hug, and pulls me in close.

"I'm sorry," I reply. "It's just. . . a shock to see your daddy after so long. . ."

"Well, he won't be back, that's for sure," Sparrow replies. "Not unless he wants his butt kicked by Daniel."

"I hope so," I reply as Sparrow grabs a box of tissues off the old vanity I'd brought along, handing me a handful. "You know, even after

all he's done, a part of me wanted to let him stay."

"Well, I'm glad you didn't," Sparrow replies. "What he did was slimy, and he doesn't deserve you or anyone. Besides, he's in trouble with the law, and you don't want that kind of trouble."

"No, I suppose I don't," I say with a nod. "It's just... hard. I've spent the past—almost thirty years with someone... and now I'm all alone." "You aren't all alone, Mama," Sparrow insists. "You have me, Daniel, and Jade just a few roads away."

"I know, but that's not what I mean," I say with a sigh. "You have your own lives, and I'm used to having a companion, you know?"

"Yeah, I get it," Sparrow says, quiet for a moment as if she's unsure of what to say. But then suddenly, she perks up. "What about that app?" "Love and Company?" I ask.

"Yeah! Have you tried it out?"

"No, I haven't actually," I reply. "I just don't think it's for me. Not right now."

"Why do you say that?" Sparrow asks.

"I think how I reacted and felt when I just merely saw your father today tells me I have no business being on there," I reply. "It wouldn't be right to just thrust myself out there when I'm not ready.

"Is anyone truly ready to move on?" Sparrow asks with a shrug. "It's hard but you've got to do it sometime."

"Little bird, I chewed out some poor guy at the store that ran into me just because he was a man," I say with shame at just the thought of it.

"Yikes," Sparrow replies.

"It was absolutely embarrassing," I reply, sniffling. "How am I supposed to just move on or do anything like that when I can't even handle being around men?"

"It's okay Mama, I'm sorry. Listen, you don't have to be ready for that," Sparrow replies. "I already told you it's not just for dating, it's for friends too. You don't have to use it to find a new partner, I'm sorry I pushed."

"It's alright. I know you mean well, sugar, but..." I trail off and try to hold back the tears. "I feel like I can't trust anybody besides you, little Joe, and Daniel now."

"Oh, Mama..." Sparrow replies with a frown.

"The man that I gave my heart to, the one that I thought had my back and I was supposed to be with forever just... crushed me. And

then seeing him again today just further proved to me that I'm still a wreck over it. I'm not sure any new 'friends' are going to want to

deal with that."

"That's not true," Sparrow replies. "I'm sure there are plenty of other women out there that will get it," Sparrow insists. "You should

create a profile and find yourself some girlfriends. I'm sure there are other people in the area who have been through a lot of what

you're going through."

"You really think so?" I ask as I pat my eyes with a tissue.

"Of course," Sparrow says with a smile.

"I haven't really tried to make friends in years, not anyone besides from work anyways," I reply with a shrug. "I always just hung out

with your father when we had time."

"See? That's precisely why you really should get out there and find some cool people to chill with," Sparrow replies. "New people with

new ideas, new ways of living that maybe will help you want to get out and experience the world."

"That... actually sounds nice," I say as she swoops back in for another hug, and as she holds me tight, there's a knock at the door.

"Hey, sorry to bother you guys, but Jade's getting really tired," Daniel says as he pokes his head in.

"Yeah, she definitely was far too busy being a hellion to nap today," Sparrow replies and stands up. "We better get going, Mama."

"That's alright. I don't want my little Jade bug to get cranky," I say as I stand up and walk them out, peppering grumpy little Jade's

cheeks with kisses until I get her to giggle.

"We will see you soon, okay?" Sparrow says as she's walking out the door, Daniel already at the car. "And remember, check out that

app! There's plenty of fish in the sea, friends or otherwise."

"Alright," I say with a nod as I close the door behind her, and I watch out the window as the lights on their van light up, slowly backing

away until they're out on the road and they disappear from sight.

Immediately, as I step away from the window, I'm hit with a gripping sensation of loneliness that makes me start to cry again as I clean up the table from dessert. Then comes the anger, the bitterness, and the sadness all rolled up into one as I slam my hand on the wood.

How could he do this to me? To us! And then, after he messes it all up, he has the nerve to come to my home and ask for a place to rest his head? Unbelievable! What a sad sack of crap!

I'm a hurricane of emotions as I finish up cleaning and decide to take a shower, realizing there are still bits of blueberry in my strawberry blonde locks. I wash it really well before I blow it dry, put on my silk cap, and hop into my pj's, dragging myself into my lonely bed.

I'm so tired, exhausted even, but the sandman isn't on my side tonight. I toss and turn, trying to get comfortable, but my mind is a buzzing whir that just won't shut up. The events of the day replaying over and over in my head.

Annoyed, I grab my phone and decide to look up the weather for tomorrow when my finger slips and accidentally hits that blasted pink heart on my screen, pulling up the Love and Company app.

"Dang it," I grunt in irritation, but as I go to swipe it away, I pause for a moment. Maybe Sparrow is right. I don't have to be lonely. I can just make a couple friends in the area, maybe some other women who've been hurt. Maybe we can be as close as the Golden Girls even!

Except, maybe without all the sass. But instead of making my profile, I lose my nerve, sighing as I put my phone down and stare at the ceiling.

I don't need some sort of app to make friends, I think to myself. *I can make them at work. There's also no need to get caught up in anything serious either, that's for sure.*

I mean, I have never known the touch of another man, and even though I feel starved in that department. . . I'd rather feel like this than get hurt like that again. Like I still am. Missing and pining over a fool who didn't know what he had. Beating myself up, wondering if it really was my fault for months and months. . .

No thanks.

I'll figure it out on my own. I don't need some computer mumbo-jumbo to help me figure out who I'd be best suited for, friends or

otherwise. That sort of stuff will fall into place organically.

As for men? I don't even want to look at another one right now, let alone make friends with them.

Chapter Six

ELI

"Ya!" I yell as I flick the reins on my stallion, working with Mitch and the boys to round up some cattle that had wandered off the

property. When I look up to see what the other three are doing, I see Mitch sitting on his horse, zoned into the job, a flat look on his

face. Something has seemed off for a few days, to be honest. In the month that he's been here at the ranch, Mitch has made life, well,

interesting. He's always joking around and smiling, chatting my ear off while we are trying to get work done, which I suppose I don't

mind at all.

But he's withdrawn all of a sudden, and it's got me worried. Problem is, I'm unsure of how to broach the subject, and I try to wrack my

brain for a way to slip it in once we get all the cows back to where they should be.

"Hey Noah, Zack?" I call out once we get all the cattle back in the pen.

"Yeah?" Noah calls out.

"Can you check on the pigs? I don't know if they've been slopped yet, and Eugenia is about ready to pop," I reply.

"Sure thing," Noah says.

"Should I check on Molly then?" Zack asks, referring to one of our mama cows that's also about ready to have her babies too.

"Uh, yeah, that'd probably be good," I reply with a nod as I hop off Whistler, and start leading him back to the horse barn, Mitch quietly following along. I wait for a moment to check if I'm wrong, waiting for him to start yammering away. But there's nothing but awkward silence.

"So, everything alright?" I ask finally as we both walk our horses in and get them settled in their pens.

"What do you mean?" Mitch asks, barely showing any emotion and sounding tired. In fact, now that I'm closer to him, I can see the bags under his eyes, purplish in color.

"You've been out of it lately," I press, and Mitch stands there for a moment, his eyes flickering toward the hay-covered floor.

"It's nothing really. . . just been dealing with some things, is all," Mitch says with a shrug. "Nothing to worry about."

"Doesn't seem like nothing," I insist, and Mitch's eyes look into mine for a moment before looking away again.

"It's not your problem, Eli," he replies. "I'll figure it out, it's just hard right now."

"Are you in some sort of trouble?" I ask, and Mitch heaves a heavy sigh, appearing to be embarrassed as his cheeks redden a little.

"I lost the house," Mitch replies.

"What?" "Well, I told you I was behind on some things, but. . . it's worse than I let on," Mitch says as he shoves his hands in his pockets and leans against a pole. "I tried my best to dig myself out of it, I tried explaining my wife had died, I did everything I could. . . but the bank doesn't care about all that."

"I feel awful, Mitch. Why didn't you tell me?" I ask.

"Because we'd only just met, I didn't want to leave a bad impression," Mitch says with a shrug.

"Wait. . . if you lost your house, where are you staying?" I decide to prod. Mitch seems wildly uncomfortable with me asking, but unfortunately, I have a feeling I already know the answer.

"In my car," he replies quietly, confirming my assumptions. "Not much else I can do unless I want to move back home. . . and I can't do

that. I don't think I'll ever be able to go back home. . ."

He clears his throat, and I can tell he's getting really upset, trying to ground himself. I feel terrible, and there's no way I can let this man

who is trying so hard to rebuild his life live out there in his car.

And then it dawns on me.

"You know, I have extra room in the house," I say, and Mitch looks at me like I've got two heads.

"Really? You'd do that for me?" Mitch asks.

"Sure, why not?" I ask. "It's really no trouble."

"Well, you hardly know me," Mitch says, but I just shrug my shoulders.

"I know you well enough, and I can't be having my ranch hand sleeping out there on the streets," I reply. "Wouldn't be right, and it

wouldn't feel right either."

"Well golly, thank you, Eli," Mitch says as he pulls his hands out of his pockets and walks toward me. I'm expecting a handshake, but

I'm caught off guard when he gives me a hug, patting my back hard before he lets go of me. "Thanks, man," Mitch says, a grin on his

face where that frown has been.

"Of course," I say, happy to see Mitch smiling again. "We can take the day tomorrow to get you settled in."

****

I wake up at the crack of dawn, yawning before kissing Mel's picture and walking out into the living room. I am surprised to find the

couch empty, besides the blankets Mitch had used for the night, folded neatly on the back. I expected he'd still be asleep.

Must be that he went to get his stuff, I thought to myself as I heard the front door creak open and slam shut, then the sound of Mitch

cussing under his breath.

"You alright out there?" I call out, walking into the kitchen.

"Yeah, sorry about that, hands are full," Mitch says as he hiked a box up in his hands. "Did I wake you?"

"No, it's time for me to get myself around," I reply.

"I have a bunch of stuff at the storage place, but I ran out and grabbed some of my essentials, some stuff to remind me of home too.

Hope that's okay." "Of course it's okay," I reply. "I got Jeff's old room ready for you; follow me."

We walk down the hallway, and I drop the key to Jeff's room on the floor. As I go to pick it up, I hear the knob of the door nearest to

me begin to turn, and immediately, I shoot up straight.

"In here?" Mitch asks.

"No!" I snap and Mitch peeks around his box at me. "Sorry. . . I mean no. . . no, it's farther down here," I say, trying to stay calm.

He didn't open her door.

It's okay, it was only an accident. . .

No one's been in her sewing room but me since she died. Not even the boys. The idea of anyone touching or moving anything

overwhelms me. So much so that I nearly had a padlock put on it.

I've left it the way it's been since the day we lost her, and when you look in there, it's as if she's never left. Because somehow, in my

mind, if I do that, when I'm at my lowest, I can almost trick myself into feeling like she's still coming home.

"Whose room is that?" Mitch asks as we walk into Jeff's old room, and he sets his box down on the bed.

"This was my son Jeff's room," I say.

"No, I mean the room I almost went into," Mitch says. "You got so upset, and I want to make sure I didn't do something wrong."

I pause for a moment as I hand him the key to his room, unsure if I really want to talk about it.

"You didn't," I reply, forcing a smile. "You just can't go in that room, okay?"

"Okay," Mitch agrees with a little nod, a confused look on his face. But I'm content to let him be confused. At least for now. "So, this

was Jeff's room? Your oldest boy?"

"And Robert's—well, until they got older," I say with a sigh, feeling thankful that he didn't push me for more information. It's too

painful to talk about, and I'm certainly not in the mood to relive it all.

"Wait, you've got four kids?" Mitch asks, sounding a bit surprised.

"Yep! All boys," I say with a chuckle. "How about you? Got any kids of your own?"

"Two, actually, a boy and a girl," Mitch replies, and at first he smiles. But then the smile quickly fades into a frown, and his brows furrow in what I can only imagine is pain. "We uh, haven't talked much since their mama died."

"Oh," I say, "sorry to hear that."

"No worries, they'll come around eventually, I'm sure," Mitch replies, but something about it seems off to me. I know that mourning and loss can really mess people up, but for a family to break up like that after such a devastating loss, it's not only heartbreaking, but odd. But in the same spirit that Mitch hadn't been nosy about Mel, I decide to let it go. If he ever wants to tell me, he will. Until then, it's his business.

The boys wake up, and before I can say a word about Mitch, Zack slips out the door. So, Noah and I leave Mitch to get his stuff all unpacked and sorted. I see him walk back and forth from his truck a few times while we're running around on the farm, and I feel bad, trying to rush around so I have time to help him. But Eugenia finally gave birth to her piglets, and I'm caught up making sure they're okay until lunch.

"You sure you don't want any help?" I call out again as I walk back toward the house to grab something.

"Nope! Thanks, but I got it," he says, so we just go back to chorin', only taking a break to eat lunch, which Mitch opted out of. Zack still hadn't returned from his blatant ditching, but he was still young and unlike Noah, had just started getting interested in girls. So, I figured I'd leave it alone.

Dinner time rolls around, and I come inside just as Zack pulls into the driveway.

"Mitch is still here?" Zack asks.

"That's the first thing you ask after abandoning your chores all day, Casanova?" Noah shoots back, sounding annoyed. "You would know what's going on if you'd have been here."

"Wait, what?" Zack replies.

"Mitch is going to be staying here with us," I reply as we walk inside, and I go to the fridge to start pulling stuff out to get dinner going.

"Seriously?" Zack asks, but his tone isn't one of excitement but of concern. I stop in my tracks and turn around to face the boys, a bit surprised by Zack's poor reaction to the news.

"Yeah," I reply. "You make it sound like it's a bad thing."

"Dad, we don't know this guy from Adam," Zack replies. "What if he's some looney tune?"

"He's got a point," Noah chimes in. "I mean he's only been here what, a month? Barely?"

"I understand what you boys are saying, but we need to keep in mind what the Lord would want us to do," I say. "God would want us to help someone in need, and Mitch is in need. He lost his wife and his home."

"Oh. . ." Zack replies, the worried look on his face slipping into a sad one. "I didn't know."

"Well, he's a man, Zack," I reply. "It's not like he's going to advertise it. Shoot, I didn't even know how bad it was 'til yesterday when I offered for him to stay here."

"So, does that mean Becky can come move in too?" Noah jokes, his attention at trying to lighten the mood.

"Haha, very funny," I say as I roll my eyes. "That's a little bit of a different situation."

"I don't know Dad, her parents are kind of a pain," Noah insists, and my only response is an annoyed groan.

"I was wondering why he was on the couch this morning," Zack says, still looking like he feels awful. Out of all the kids, Zack had always seemed to take it the hardest when his mama died. He'd been a big time Mama's boy, and when she was taken from us, for a long time he wasn't right.

Lately, he's finally coming into his own, which has been lovely. But as he sits there with that dejected look on his face, I wonder if Mitch's story has stirred up the past in his mind.

"Well, now you know," I say. "He's in Jeff's old room, and I'd appreciate it if all of us could be understanding of Mitch's situation and welcoming, just like people were with us."

"Yes sir," Noah and Zack reply, Zack's face lightening up a bit just in time for Mitch to come out.

"Need a hand with dinner?" Mitch asks.

"Sure," I say as I hand him a cutting board, a knife, and veggies to chop. "Going to make some fajitas."

"Ooh! My favorite!" Mitch says cheerfully as he sits down and begins to slice things up. The four of us chat amongst ourselves,

shooting the breeze and getting to know one another better.

Dinner is delicious as usual—thanks to me—and after dinner the boys take off to their rooms after we clean up, leaving Mitch and I

alone to hang out in the living room. I take a seat in my worn-out armchair and turn on the TV as Mitch sort of wanders around the

room, seeming to be scoping the place out.

He stops short of the mantle as he inspects the picture there, picking up the picture frame in his hands. I know what's coming, and my

heart drops into my stomach as he opens his mouth to speak.

"Ooh wee! Who's the vixen here with you and your boys?" Mitch asks, and I find myself struggling to keep myself together enough to

answer.

"That's my wife, Melanie," I say.

"Oh! Well, where is she?" Mitch asks, appearing to be confused.

"She... she's no longer with us," I reply, my voice cracking a little bit.

"Oh no... I'm so sorry, Eli, I didn't know," Mitch says. "I would have never said that."

"It's okay," I say after clearing my throat. "It's not like you're wrong, she was ethereal, like an angel, you know?"

"Definitely," Mitch agrees as he puts the picture back down. "She was gorgeous."

"She sure was," I say with a half-smile.

"I hope this ain't too forward, but what happened?" Mitch asked, and my blood chills. I knew eventually this conversation would

happen. I have plenty of pictures of Melanie everywhere, family pictures too. So, I might as well finally tell him what happened.

"She got killed in a car accident," I reply. "It was a really rainy, autumn night. So, it was already a bit slippery out there from the leaves and the wetness on the roads. She was going to turn onto the road that comes up this way from town, and some jackass in a sports car was drunk. Slammed on his breaks, but not in time... so he smashed right into her as she was turning."

"Jesus," Mitch replies quietly. "I'm so sorry. How long has she been gone?"

"A decade now, about when I hired you, actually," I reply. "It was hard. Still is."

"I can imagine," Mitch replies. "That's not something you can easily get over."

"No, it ain't," I agree. "I wish I could say it gets easier and give you a bit of comfort... but I've just learned to live with it because that's

what she would have wanted. For me to keep going."

"I guess that is all you can do," Mitch agrees with his head hung low as he sits down on the couch next to me, and I flip the channels

on the TV. "Golly, ten years is a long time."

"Sure is," I say as the TV flickers with each press of the button. "I'm sorry for how I acted earlier by the way. That was her sewing room."

"No need to apologize," Mitch insists.

"She liked to make quilts and such and sell them at the farmer's market. She was just starting to really get going online but then

Emmett Gaines took that all away."

"Did they do anything to him?" Mitch asked.

"No," I reply, my jaw clenching as a streak of anger rises up, and I take a deep breath before I go on to quell it best I can. "He was the

sheriff's son. I'm sure you can guess how that played out."

"Ugh, disgusting," Mitch replies, and a deafening silence fills the room for a while as I settle on an old John Wayne movie. We watch it

for a while, and I try my best not to think about the feelings the conversation has drummed up.

The sadness, the anger. The rage I'd felt when I'd nearly catapulted over the barrier in the courthouse when they'd given that little jerk

probation, rehab, and AA meetings. All while my beautiful wife lay six feet under. Unlike Emmett, Mel would never get a second

chance. But money and who you know seems to speak loudest. At least, that's what I've come to learn.

"You know, I don't want to step on your toes," Mitch says. "But have you considered that maybe what you need to do is let loose and move on?"

I shoot him a look of surprise. *He's just lost his wife himself, so why would he suggest something like that, knowing how I feel?*

"No, never," I say.

"But you said Mel would want you to be happy, right?" Mitch asks.

"Well. . . yeah," I reluctantly agree.

"A friend suggested this app for me, it's called Love and Company," Mitch says. "It's not just for dating, you can make friends on there

too. . . I'm not ready, but I mean, it's been a decade. I'd just hate to see you live the rest of your life lonely, Eli. Especially after all you're

doing for me."

"I don't know, I just think I'm better off alone," I reply. "I mean, Melanie was the love of my life. I could never replace her."

"Of course not," he says. "But I do know one thing, it's not healthy for a man to grieve forever. You deserve happiness."

"I am happy," I insist, which is mostly true. "I miss Mel like the dickens, but I have four boys that love me, and I see most of them often

—except Robert. He went off to California to be a personal trainer, trying to rub elbows with the stars I guess. But I've got the farm, the

animals. . . I'm content."

"But there's still that hole, right?" Mitch asks, and I'm not sure how to answer his question. There is one, but I don't think just anyone

can fill it, nor do I think some app is going to magically solve it either. "Listen, my friend did find someone else on this thing after his

wife died."

"I'm not really into computers, Mitch," I reply with a shrug. "Not my forte. The only thing I use a computer for is my emails, business

stuff, and my taxes."

"But you've got a smartphone, right?" Mitch asks.

"Well sure, of course I do," I reply with a nod. "I'm getting old, but I'm no fossil," I say with a chuckle.

"Then you should put yourself out there on that app," Mitch replies. "I'm telling ya, it's real easy to use."

"So, you've tried it?" I ask, raising an eyebrow, finding it a bit weird that he'd already checked it out, but trying desperately not to judge.

"Not exactly," Mitch replies. "I made a profile and such but nothing major. I mean, it's only been a year since I lost Darlene... but I know someday I will. Because I know that, like Mel, Darlene would want me to be happy. Darlene told me so herself."

"Hmm," I say with a little nod as Mitch gets up, stretches, and begins to yawn. "Sorry to gab and run, but I'm beat."

"It's alright, I should get to bed soon myself," I say.

"Just consider what I said, alright?" Mitch replies.

"Yeah, sure," I say with a nod as Mitch walks out of the hallway, his footfalls echoing in the quiet house, followed by his door clicking closed.

Maybe he's got something there, I think as I sit in my chair, hands gripped into the arms of it. *It has been a decade, the boys are growing up, soon it'll be an empty nest here I reckon. Well, unless I hire and board more workers...*

I pull my phone out of my breast pocket, look up the app on the store, and wait for it to download. The whole while that I watch the little downloading line tick closer and closer, I can feel myself getting anxious.

What am I doing? I ask myself. *Isn't doing this like spitting on Mel's grave? She was my everything... Am I really ready to do this?*

As I wrestle with myself, I remember a conversation we'd had one night. The stars in the sky had twinkled big and bright as we talked about the future while Zack and Noah were cooking in her belly—though we didn't know quite yet that we were having twins.

She'd said to me that if anything ever happened to her, she'd want me to live. She would want me to take care of the boys and be happy, and if that meant finding someone new, then it did.

At the time, I'd laughed it off, kissed her, and told her that's never going to happen. But never came, and now, I'm thinking Mitch might be right. *It's unhealthy for a man to grieve as long as I have.*

I make a profile, answer a gaggle of silly questions that they say will help match you to your perfect mate, and I take a selfie to upload.

CHAPTER SIX   47

But when I go to put the picture up, it refuses to load.

Guess I'll have to do that later, I think to myself, heading off to bed. *I'm not sure that I'll even find anyone on there interesting enough to catch my eye,* I think to myself as I look out the window. But I suppose it might be nice to have a woman's touch around here again.

Chapter Seven

Skylar White
Clean Romance

Darla

Another sleepless, frustrating night, I think to myself as I watch TV, trying to find something to hopefully bore myself asleep.

Tomorrow's my first day at the new hospital, Thistleberry General, and though I'm nervous about the new gig, that's not the only thing

keeping me up. Ever since Joseph showed up, I've been a wreck. Thankfully, Sparrow and the gang have been busy with other things,

otherwise, they'd see the wads of tissues all over my dresser and my swollen eyes from crying. Or the takeout containers haphazardly

sprawling out of my wastebasket.

I had accepted it all. All the pain of losing the animals. All the pain from losing him. But when he showed up, so arrogant, thinking I'd

taken him back, it had really messed me up. More than I thought it would, to be honest.

His words had been like him taking his fingers, sinking them into my flesh, and prying those scars apart. Every rip from his words

leaving me bloody and bruised all over again. The memory of finding him and that girl in our bed replaying in my mind, and all my emotions about it resurfacing and surging like a raging typhoon, destroying me mentally all over again.

I can't live my life like this forever, I think to myself as I get up to use the bathroom. *I am starting fresh, and even though it's not quite the way I thought life was going to go, it's still my life. So why not make the best of it?*

After using the restroom, I make it back to the bedroom, eyeing the phone lying there in its pink case on my nightstand. I grasp it in

my hand as I turn the screen on and ignore the nerves creeping up.

Sparrow is right. There's no reason to sit here and dwell on what once was. *All I have is right here, and right now... and I want to love in the moment before it passes me by.*

I decide to go through the whole process of starting a profile, and once my login is set up, I'm surprised at how in depth it all is. I'm

asked the normal questions I assumed it would—name, birthday, where I'm from, what I do for a living—but then it asked some other questions.

What music do you like?

What movies do you like?

If you were on a desert island, what would you bring with you?

Then came the multiple-choice questions. Everything from political alignments to physical preferences—which, though a lot of them

didn't apply for me, seemed like a nice touch—and a whole bunch of other stuff. In fact, by the end of it all, I was surprised at how

intuitive it all seemed to be. It was like it was asking everything under the sun to try to push you toward like-minded people.

While the rest of the questions were sort of fun, the final question gave me pause.

What are you looking for?

What am I looking for, exactly? I ask myself. *I'm definitely not looking for a relationship. That'll just get my heart broken all over again.*

And how many people are really going to be on here that aren't looking for a relationship or a one-night stand? Probably not many.

No! I scold myself. *I'm not going to be pessimistic! I am going to put myself out there!* So, under the question, I put friends and maybe

something more, leaving myself open to whatever happens to go with the flow. *Seems like a good enough answer as any.*

The app then pops up a prompt to add a picture, and immediately, I feel my anxiety kick in. *I'll have to take something tomorrow when

I'm all made up,* I think to myself. And so, I click 'do this later, and the app announces I'm all done with fancy little stars and fireworks,

telling me that I'm 'ready to make friends!'

Huh, that was easier than I thought, I think to myself as I look at the time. *Jeez, it's already one in the morning? I'll have to check this out

later.* However, as I put my phone down, my phone begins to ping over and over again.

Worried that it was Sparrow or little Joe, I pick up my phone, only to see the notifications are from the app. "Eh, I'll just read these in

the morning," I say to myself, yawning as I turn down the TV and lay my head against the pillow.

A few minutes later, my phone is more alive than it ever has been, and I sit up and put my glasses back on. Curiosity getting the best

of me, I pick up my phone once again, and I'm shocked to see all the notifications are from all different people—male and female—

filling up my Love and Company inbox.

Sheesh, that was fast! I think to myself as I poke the app button and start scrolling through the messages. One is from a slightly

younger woman, Sheila, who had also been cheated on and wants to get to know me. It honestly sounded lovely; I really do need

friends. There's another email from a guy named Butch, who is asking for my picture, and I tell him I'm tired and I'll put one up

tomorrow. But he persists, so I put his chat on 'ignore'. *Too pushy.*

I then open the next one, only to gasp, shocked and wanting to soak my eyes in bleach as I'm greeted with a picture of some man's...

well... ding-a-ling. I surely didn't want to see that.

"Friggin' animals," I say as I block the phallic phantom, nearly putting the phone down as my stomach lurches in disgust.

But then there's a message that comes through from a man, his handle says 'TheRanchman', and it piques my interest. *A rancher, huh?*

I think to myself as I click on his profile first, wary of just opening his message.

There's no picture, which is a bit disappointing, but I can't really be too upset about that. I mean, I don't have one up either.

He's fifty-four, and he runs a ranch just outside of San Antonio, not far from me. As I read, the way he talks about his love for animals

and life on the ranch pulls me in, reminding me of the love I'd had for Laney and the rest of my animals. . . an obvious common

interest. He likes country music and some classic rock.

Check.

He loves gardening and cooking. *Check and check.*

The more I go through and read his questions, the more I realize how alike we really are. . . and the app agrees, surprising me with a

ninety-two percent compatibility rating.

Still a bit wary that I'll be blasted in the eyes with another dirty photo, I cautiously open his message, only to find that there's none to

be found.

Good evening. The message begins. *Well, morning, I suppose. My apologies for the late message. I couldn't sleep, and then it suggested you as a friend. So, I figured, why not?*

Well, he sounds just as nervous as I am, I think to myself. But he sounds like a gentleman so far.

Hello! I reply back. *It's okay, I couldn't sleep either.*

Dang, what was that one thing Sparrow told me to use when I wanted to express laughing or something? Oh, right! An emoji!

So, I search through the little pictures under the smiling face and pick out one that's laughing.

Good, I'm glad I didn't offend, he replies, a smiley face punctuating the end of his sentence. *So, I'm going to be honest, I don't know how to go about this. I'm not too good with technology.*

You and me both, I reply with another laughing face, and he sends one back.

My name's Eli, but I suppose you saw that in my profile. I'm looking to make friends first, then see where it goes.

Me too! I reply, and for the next hour or so, Eli and I text back and forth, shooting the breeze—albeit a bit awkwardly. But it's not weird

awkward, more like endearing. We talk about ranch life, animals, and what movies and music we like. Then we gab a bit about TV and

how we miss the old shows and find ourselves watching old stuff over and over.

Both of us have kids, though he's got double the amount I do. But it doesn't bother me at all. From the way he talks, he's got nothing
but love for his boys.

Four of them! I typed. *I don't know that I could survive! Little Joe and Sparrow were enough!* I say, and it makes him laugh.

At first, I worry that he'll ask where their father is, but he doesn't. And though my brain is nagging at me to ask where his ex is, out of
respect, I don't.

If I don't want my can of worms opened—an embarrassing one at that—it wouldn't be right to insist on knowing his.

Before I know it, when I glance over to the clock, it's nearly three a.m., and my eyes widen as I remember I need to get some sleep
since orientation is at noon later that day at the hospital.

I hate to cut this short, but I start work tomorrow, and I need to at least attempt to sleep, I say.

That's alright, he replies. *I have to get up to start chorin' myself by eight at the latest, and I usually eat breakfast at six.*

Oh no, I hope I didn't keep you awake! I reply, feeling bad that I didn't figure he'd have to get up much earlier than I did.

Don't worry darlin', he replies. *If anything, the boys and Mitch will have to give me a little leeway.*

Darlin', huh? I think to myself with a crooked little smile. I like that. A lot actually.

Hey, before you go, Eli types. *I was wondering if maybe you'd like to go out sometime. Coffee first, maybe? I'd like to get to know you better, and while the app is nice, I'm better face-to-face.*

I pause for a moment, my fingers hovering over the little electronic keyboard in front of me. I want to say yes, he seems so awesome.

But admittedly, I'm scared. I'm still a wounded animal, trying to heal. Would it really be fair to drag someone else into that nonsense?

I should be more focused on work, right?

All these thoughts swirl in my head for a moment, but I shake them all off. There's something about Eli that just feels... different. I
can't explain it, and I don't think I need to label it, at least not right now. But I feel like I need to give him a chance.

CHAPTER SEVEN 53

How does Wednesday morning sound? I ask. *It's my next day off.*

That sounds perfect, he says with a smiley face next to it, and I feel my face get a little warm as I smile too. *It's been lovely talking to you, Darla,* he says, and the warmth deepens.

It's been lovely speaking with you too, Eli, I reply.

Eight o'clock at the state diner on Cliff Street? Eli asks. *That way, if you decide you want a little breakfast or something, there's the option.*

That would be great! I say.

Alright, well, don't be a stranger, Eli says with a winking face.

Don't worry, I won't, I reply as I let out a contented sigh and put down my phone, finally lying down for the night. A big grin sits on

my face as I stare at the TV, excited for the future.

As the adrenaline and excitement wear off, and I gently slip off to sleep, I find myself dreaming of the cowboy I'm going to meet.

Wondering if this will be the end of my streak of bad luck.

I truly hope so. Because he sounds like a dreamboat.

***

After a night full of dreams of riding through the field on horses with Mr. Eli, I make myself breakfast—eggs, bacon, cottage cheese,

and toast—and sit down at the table to eat. All the while, Eli remains in my thoughts.

I feel like a dumb teenager, being so excited about Wednesday. But he seems so funny, kind, and genuine. A true gentleman.

Something that maybe I need in my life. Someone to show me that, like Sparrow says, every man isn't bad.

Even if it doesn't go anywhere, it'd be nice to have another friend, at least. Though a big part of me is excited and hoping that it will

lead somewhere, which is funny since just a few days ago, I was so against even trying.

I take a shower, get dressed in my favorite pair of scrubs, and eye the clock. I still have plenty of time before work, so I decide to put

on my face, feeling really good about myself.

Towels piled on my head, I did my eye makeup and worked my way to my lips when I heard a knock at the door. Maybe it's the

mailman, I think to myself. He knocked on Friday when we dropped off a package.

I go to the door, still in my robe, and when I open it, I'm immediately filled with rage as I'm face-to-face with my past once more.

"Apparently, I didn't make myself clear enough the last time you showed up," I say as Joe stands there with a fistful of roses in his

hand. "I brought you something," Joseph says as my eyes flicker toward the flowers and then back to him.

"I don't like roses. I like lilies," I reply. "Not that you'd possibly remember."

"Darla, come on now, don't be difficult," Joseph replies, his smile unwavering despite my obviously grumpy demeanor.

"You're the one who is being difficult," I growl. "Because apparently you don't understand the meaning of 'don't come back here'."

"Oh, don't be like that, sweetheart," Joseph says, and the very word 'sweetheart' coming out of his mouth makes me nauseous.

"Don't you patronize me," I reply. "I had nothing to say to you the other day, and I surely have got nothing to say to you now."

"But I love you, Darla," he whines, and I'm hit with the acrid and strong smell of booze.

"Ugh! Have you been drinking?"

"That doesn't matter," Joseph says. "What matters is I love you—"

"Don't," I say as I feel my chest tighten and my eyes begin to burn.

"Don't what?"

"Don't say that to me," I reply. "Because if you did, if you ever had, you wouldn't have done what you did. And if you respected me,

you wouldn't be here at my doorstep all over again."

"That's not true!" he insists, and he takes a step forward. Heart pounding, I try to slam the door shut, but it won't close. His boot is

wedged in between the door and the frame.

"Joe, move your foot! Now!' I yell. "I don't want you anywhere near me!"

"Come on now, you don't mean that, Darla," Joseph says. "I need a place to go, and what better place to go than back into the arms of my lover?"

"I do!" I scream back. "I don't want anything to do with your cheesy, drunk, cheating, low down, dirty, and no good pathetic self!"

I insist, and his smile fades; I can see the rage begin to filter into his eyes. "You are not welcome here."

"Who do you think you are?" Joseph spits. "You think you can just talk to me like that?"

"Truth hurts, doesn't it?" I reply. "Now leave before I call the cops."

"You wouldn't," Joseph replies, glaring at me.

"Try me," I say, glaring right back, holding stern even though I am scared out of my wits, and I feel like my heart's going to explode.

I've never seen him so angry. "You wouldn't do well in jail, Joe," I continue, steeling my nerves, wanting to drive it home in his brain to

leave me be.

"This isn't over, Darla," Joseph says as he slides his boot out from the door, and I quickly close it, deadbolting and locking it before I

run to the window in time to hear his engine rev and his tires squeal as he speeds off. I'm left wondering if his words were talk or if he

meant it.

Chapter Eight

ELI

I hiss as I nick my skin a little with my razor, my hands shaking slightly as I do my best to spruce myself up for my coffee date with

Darla. A part of me is excited, but there's another part of me that is absolutely terrified.

Maybe this isn't the best idea. I think to myself as I press a piece of toilet paper to the tiny wound, the blood blooming slowly through

the other side of the thin, ivory-white tissue. *I mean, Darla seems like a sweetheart and all, but I'm not sure I'm ready for this. I should call this whole thing off...*

It still feels like yesterday that Melanie was playing Stevie Nick's in the kitchen, twirling around while she cut roses from her prized

bushes. The fragrance carried all through the house, and every time I came in from work, she'd be there with a smile and a kiss.

Sometimes, when I think of her, I can almost feel her fingertips on my skin...

The phone buzzes, and it brings me back to reality. It's me, staring at myself alone in the mirror, my phone going off again. I pick it up,

and there she is. Darla. And even in my bout of self-doubt, somehow Darla seems to pull me out of it.

Hey! Just wanted to confirm the address for the coffee place :)

I can't help but smile. I haven't even seen her yet, but there's something about her that really draws me in. Maybe it's because she and I have so much in common, or maybe because I'm just that lonely. Honestly, I can't be too sure. But the part of me that wants to find out wins over the fear, and I text her back the address before shoving my phone in my breast pocket and heading to the kitchen.

"Ooh wee!" Noah yips as I walk in. "Looking mighty fine there, Pops."

"Where are you headed to?" Zack asks.

"If you must know, I'm headed out for coffee with a friend," I reply, and the two boys let out a low gasp.

"No way," Noah says. "You're going out on a date?"

"Mmm," I say, "something like that."

"Come on, boys, don't give your daddy such a hard time," Mitch insists. "But a bolo tie? Really?"

"What's wrong with my bolo tie?" I ask, and they all look at one another before they burst into laughter. "I think she'll like it! She likes the cowboy look."

"Well, then, maybe it'll work in your favor," Mitch says with a grin.

"Hope so," I say, feeling my nerves creep up a bit.

"Eli, I'm sure you're gonna do fine," Mitch replies, leaning back in his chair. "We will hold down the fort here. You go have fun."

"Thanks, Mitch," I say as I go to open the door. "I owe ya one."

"Nah, I'd say we're even," Mitch replies with a wink, flicking the toothpick in his mouth to the other side. "I'm just glad you took my advice! Now go on before you're late!"

"O-oh, yeah, right," I say as I hurry out, the heavy storm door clattering behind me as I get in my truck and start it up.

"You can do this," I give myself a pep talk as I rev the engine, looking at myself in the rearview mirror, setting my sunglasses on the bridge of my nose. "You deserve it."

All the way there my hands are clammy and sweaty, so much so that I have to stop for a second to dry them, so they stop sliding all over the steering wheel. *If this is what I'm supposed to do to move on. . . why do I feel so guilty?* I ask myself. Even though Mel herself told me that she wanted me to be happy, and Mitch told me she probably wouldn't want me to be lonely, it still feels like seeing another woman is like cheating.

But how do you cheat on someone who's long gone?

The drive feels like it's taking forever, but as I pull into the parking lot, it suddenly doesn't feel like it was long enough.

I sit there for a moment, staring at the place with my door on the handle, once again wondering if I should just turn back. But it

wouldn't be right to leave a lady waiting, so I take a deep breath, open the door, and head inside.

I get inside and take off my sunglasses, folding them up and setting them on my collar as I scan the room. I'm looking for a blonde in

a red, polka-dotted dress, and I quickly find her in the furthest back booth like we'd discussed.

As I walk closer, her features become more defined as she looks at a menu. Her pouty red lips are the first thing I notice before

realizing she's all dressed up, her blonde hair curly and her lashes long and fluttery.

She finally looks up, and I freeze in place as our eyes lock on one another's. Where there were once butterflies, I'm hit with a horrifying realization.

The pin-up look.

Those eyes. . . affixed in a horrified look as she stares at me.

It's the crazy pie lady! You've got to be kidding me. . .

* * *

"E-Eli?" I ask, my voice quivering, recognizing him instantly. *How is this happening right now? I ask myself. It's the guy from the grocery store that ran into me!* But if he knows it, he doesn't show it as he steps closer and reaches his hand out toward mine.

"Yep, that's me," he says with a smile. "And you must be Darla."

Maybe he forgot, I tell myself, trying to calm myself down. *I mean, he couldn't have gotten that good of a look at me, right?*

"Mm-hmm, that's me," I say as I take his hand in mine, and I'm surprised when he gives it a gentlemanly peck, causing heat to crawl up my neck as he lets go and sits down across from me.

"Nice to see that they were able to clean up that dress for you," Eli says.

Aw crap, he does remember, I think to myself as my stomach does flip-flops. *Lucky me.*

"Yes! Well, the guy said I did the right thing by getting some dawn dish soap on it immediately."

"He's a miracle worker," Eli says with a chuckle, his smile crinkling the corners of his eyes.

"Sure is," I say with a smile.

It's awkwardly and unnervingly quiet for a moment as he fidgets with the salt and pepper shakers before picking up a menu from the basket on the side. His eyes scan it, and I bite my lip as I look down at my own, unsure of what to say.

This is so much different than being behind a screen. . . all that false confidence is gone. And now that I know, he knows I'm the pie girl. . .

"Well, y-you look beautiful," Eli stammers, and I realize quickly that he's just as nervous as I am. *Maybe the pie thing isn't such a big deal,* I think to myself as I sit up straight. I want to ooze confidence. First impressions may be everything, but maybe I can redeem myself.

"You know, I am truly sorry about all of that," I say. "I was having a really bad day."

"I kind of figured when you told me off on behalf of mankind," Eli says with a chuckle.

"Ugh, I'm so embarrassed," I reply with a snort, feeling the tension ease up a little. "It really had nothing to do with you; my ex showed up, and, well, it didn't go well." *Alright, Darla, reel in the ex-talk. If he can joke about it, so can I.* "But hey, at least you're not a bad egg."

"Mm-hmm," he says, and I realize that it's possible that he's just playing nice for niceness's sake. "They do say, though, that one bad egg spoils the whole bunch."

"Well, so far you don't seem like spoiled goods," I insist, and Eli laughs.

"I suppose not, but I suppose time will tell, huh?" Eli replies, and I'm not sure what he means, but I'm taking it as a good omen. I mean, if he wasn't at all interested, he wouldn't be sitting here still, would he? If it were me and I saw the lady that cursed me out in a store over a pie, I might run.

But not Eli. He's. . . different.

We order our coffee, and by the time it gets there, we both realize that we're starving.

"What's good here?" I ask.

"Well, everything is good to be honest," Eli says. "But I always settle for the sunny side-ups with bacon, sausage, and toast."

"Hmm. . ." I say as I look at the menu again. "I don't know, these fruit covered waffles sound good."

"The Belgians? Yeah, they're pretty great," Eli says. "Best around, I'd say. Nothing like that I-Flop."

We both laugh as the waitress comes back around, and we order our food. It's not perfect by any means—we are both still a bit nervous—but I don't want this to end up a disaster for either of us.

"So, your ranch," I say as I push through a bit of silence. "How long have you had it?"

"Mmm. . . well, I'm fifty-four, so. . ." Eli pauses for a moment to think, and while he does I can't help but notice how handsome he is. For fifty-four, he sure doesn't look it. His tanned skin making him look like a golden God. And though he has flecks of white in his dark, ebony hair, he still doesn't look a day over forty. Possibly even younger.

"I'd say about thirty years, or close to it," he replies finally. "Give or take."

"Oh wow, that's a long time," I say.

"Yeah, well, I grew up the son of a farrier, and I was just used to that sort of life, you know?" Eli says. "My daddy gave us our first little group of cows. Let me keep my horse, and we went from there."

"That's so amazing that your father would do that for you," I reply.

"Yeah, he's quite the man, I'll say," Eli says. "Now we've got so many cows, I don't know what to do with them. Then there's the horses. We got our own, and we boarded other people's horses, let them ride on the property. We have some pigs and chickens as well. . ."

"Sounds like you love animals," I reply.

"Sure do," Eli says with a nod.

"Makes me miss my little farm, before the divorce," I say, and I feel my spirits sag a little. All this talk about his animals reminding me a bit of what I'd lost.

"I'm sorry to hear that," Eli says with a frown. "How big was the farm?"

"I mean, probably small to you, but big to me," I say with a chuckle. "I had a couple of cows, a pen of chickens, no pigs. Joseph hated those."

"Joseph?"

"Oh, sorry, my ex-husband," I say, feeling embarrassed that I even brought him up again.

"Ah, I gotcha," Eli replies.

"But, uh, what I miss most is my Laney," I say with a sigh as I grip my coffee cup, and the waitress comes by with our food. "She was a full dapple gray, and so sweet."

"Those are beautiful horses for sure," Eli replies. I reach for the creamer, and as I do, he reaches for the sugar, and his hand brushes against mine, instantly sending a thrilling chill up my arm. Goosebumps pile up my arms as he shoots me a smile, and I shyly smile back.

"You know, if you ever need a boarding place, I've got you," he says.

"I'll keep that in mind," I reply, butterflies rustling through my belly.

We spend a lot of time shooting the breeze as we eat, talking about our lives, work, and everything in between. Though the beginning seemed like it was headed for a disaster since he'd recognized me as 'the pie girl', I'm delighted at how wonderfully it's going.

It's been a long time since I've talked with anyone like this, I think to myself as a faint buzzing sound comes from his direction.

"Excuse me," he says as he pulls his phone from his breast pocket. "It's one of my boys, and I got to take this."

"No worries," I say as I sit there, eating the last few bites of my waffles and fruit as he nods and talks.

"Well, just hold tight the best ya can, Zack," he says to whomever is on the phone. "I'll see you soon."

"Your son, I take it?" I ask as he hangs up the phone and puts it back in his pocket.

"Yeah, unfortunately," Eli says with a sigh. "My one cow is going into labor, and the vet had told us it may be twins. . . so Zack is nervous about me not being there."

"Oh my gosh! That is a big deal," I gasp.

"Yeah, I got to call the doc and everything, get him over there," Eli replies. "I'm just sorry I have to cut out of here early."

"Don't be," I insist. "I've had a lovely time."

"Me too," Eli says with a sigh. "Even if you did hit me with a pie the other day," he jokes with a wink, and we both end up laughing so loud the people around us stare. But I don't care. This is the happiest I've been in a long while, and they can gawk if they want to.

"You're never going to let me live that down, huh?" I ask.

"Nope," Eli says with a smirk as he gets up from the table, surprising me when he sets a hundred dollars down for our thirty-dollar bill. "You know, you should come by sometime. I got plenty of horses for you to ride if you're missing it."

"You know, I might have to take you up on that," I reply.

"Well, what are you doing on Valentine's Day?" Eli asks.

"Oh! Um, nothing really," I reply. "I mean I work 'til seven. Why?"

"Well, I was wondering if you'd want to go to dinner," Eli replies. "I know eight is a bit late, but I'd really like to take you out if you'd like to go."

"I would love to," I say with a smile as Eli puts his cowboy hat back on.

"The fourteenth at eight, then," Eli says as he tips his hat at me. "It's been a pleasure, Ms. Darla."

"Likewise," I say, and my heart pitter-patters when he smiles before he walks away. I watch him until he's out the door.

"Wow." I breathe to myself as I quickly finish my coffee and gather up my purse. *He sure is something.*

I can't help but be giddy the whole drive home, a great big smile on my face as Eli runs through my mind. I crank up the tunes on the radio, and for the first time in a long time, I actually enjoy them, singing along like a chipper little bird.

It's strange, but going out with Eli on our little breakfast excursion has caused this odd shift within me that I can't explain. And though I'm still anxious about it all and where it might lead, I can't help but feel something I hadn't felt in a long time.

Hope.

And honestly? It feels so good.

Chapter Nine

Skylar White
Clean Romance

ELI

Even though my mind is focused on helping out my prized cow and her babies, Darla is, surprisingly, still so fresh in my mind. Wandering through, a refreshing little thought in the world of mine that had become so cold and gray.

Sure, the first time we met hadn't been so hot. However, it's been a blast talking with her over text, and now that I've met her in person, it feels like the pie incident doesn't matter at all. She feels like the splash of color I might very well need. A vibrant ray of hope in my mind as I park the car and jog over to the cow, only to see Mitch come out with the vet.

"Hey, what's going on? Everything alright?" I ask as I watch the vet take off his gloves.

"False alarm," the vet says. "She's not calving, it's false labor, looks like. But it won't be that way for long."

"Thank you, Doc," I reply.

"Call me if there's anything else," the vet says as he walks past me, leaving just Mitch and I alone by the barn.

"Sorry about interrupting your date," Mitch sighs. "I tried to convince Zack we had it, but he was insistent that you come home."

"It's alright," I say with a shrug. "That's how ranch life is."

"How'd it go?" Mitch asks.

"Really good actually," I say. "Funnily enough, it was the pie girl."

"You're kidding!" Mitch replies, shocked.

"Yeah, I was surprised too," I say. "But I really think you're on to something."

"Well, I'm glad you took my advice," Mitch says with a smile. "So, what's the lucky lady's name?"

"Darla," I say as we start to walk back toward the house, but Mitch stops in his tracks.

"Darla, huh?"

"Yeah, she's new around these parts," I say, and I watch as Mitch's face seems to shift from jovial to clearly uncomfortable.

"Wouldn't happen to be Darla Middleton, would it?" Mitch asks, and I'm instantly shocked that he knew.

"Yeah, actually," I reply. "How'd you know?"

"Man, I hate to be the bearer of bad news, but Darla is no good," Mitch says, his face a tight line.

"What are you talking about?" I ask.

"I'm friends with her ex-husband, Joseph," Mitch says.

"Ah, yeah, she did say something about her ex showing up the day of the pie thing," I reply.

"Yeah well, she's not as innocent as she seems," Mitch says. "She took everything from him, got a nasty temper too."

"Well, that's not what I heard," I say, not wanting to disclose all Darla's dirty laundry. We'd sort of talked about Joseph in text messages a bit, and it wasn't my business to mouth off about.

"I'm telling ya Eli, she's known around here to be crazy." *Around here?* I think to myself. That doesn't make any since. *She just moved here... maybe he misspoke.*

"I think you're being a little biased and dramatic," I reply, defending Darla.

"She screamed at you in the middle of a store, you said so yourself," Mitch reminds me, but I just shake it off.

"She was having a bad day," I reply. "Listen, I appreciate the warning, but I like her, and I'm going to keep seeing her," I said. "I'm a big boy, I can take care of myself."

"Fine," Mitch replies, his response a confusing amalgamation of seemingly upset, frustrated... and almost angry. "But don't say I didn't warn you about that maneater."

Mitch walks past me at a quick stride and goes into the house, letting the front door nearly slam shut. *Jeez, he's really angry,* I think to myself. *His heart is in the right place, but I'm not going to listen to some dumb gossip. Especially when he's friends with the guy. He's biased, and she seems like a treasure that Joseph just threw away like a big dummy.*

I'm an adult, and I can form my own opinions about her. Frankly, I cannot wait to take her out on Valentine's Day. It may only be a few days away but dang, for some reason, it feels like it's much further than that...

***

"Earth to Darla!" Doreen says, snapping her finger playfully in my face as she breaks me out of my daydream of riding horses side by side with Eli in the morning light. The scent of fresh grass and the gleam of morning dew on the blades disintegrating as I look around at the sterile, white walls of the hospital. The smell of grass replaced by antiseptics and cleaners.

"Sorry," I say with a yawn as I begin to pick at the microwaved fajita bowl in front of me. Usually we eat in the breakroom, but today's been busy, so we are all sitting at the nurse's station, eating behind the desk.

"You have been in the clouds today," Nala says, another nurse from my coveted maternity ward spot. Working in the ICU isn't at all what I'm used to, but it'll do until I can get back on the ward myself.

Nala is a good friend of Doreen's. In fact, she's the head nurse up there, and she's snuck down to eat with us. So, I'm trying to make friends with her and ease my way into her good graces. Maybe even secure myself a transfer. Not that Doreen isn't amazing. She is. Just, the ICU is often such a bleak place to be. And I really take it hard when a patient doesn't make it.

"Well, to be honest, I met this guy," I say, and Doreen's eyes light right up. She may be my boss, but she's not a stuffy or snooty woman, and we've become fast friends.

"Oh really?" Doreen asks.

"Mm-hmm! He owns his own ranch, and he is so handsome," I say with a big grin on my face. "We went on a breakfast date, and it was really nice."

"Ooh! you got yourself a cowboy, huh?" Doreen asks.

"I sure did," I reply. "We've only just met, but he's such a gentleman. He just exudes that smoldering southern charm, you know?"

"Sounds like this guy has swept you right off your feet with the way you're gushing," Nala says, and my face immediately gets hot.

"I guess you could say that," I reply shyly.

"So, when are you going to see this tall, dark, and handsome cowboy again?" Doreen asks.

"Valentine's Day," I said. "Actually, I'm headed out with him right after work."

"That's awesome! Where are you going?" Nala asks.

"Excuse me, I'm looking for a Darla Middleton?" a man asks, wearing a delivery uniform.

"Oh, well, that's me," I say, wondering what could possibly be being delivered to me. Especially at work of all places. I wander over to the front of the desk to meet the young man, and he groans as he picks up a huge vase, full to the brim with lilies.

"What in the world. . ." I gasp, mouth agape as the fragrant scent of the flowers fills the air.

"Someone must really like you," the delivery guy says, and he thrusts a little digital pad in front of me. "Please sign here."

"O-oh! Sure!" I manage to get out, and as he leaves, I notice the card sticking out of the pot. So, I open it up and I can't help but grin as I read it out loud to myself.

"For my wild little Texas rose. . . though I suppose I should say Texas Lily, huh? Hopefully now you won't need to be throwing pies my way anymore. Sincerely, Eli."

"They're from the cowboy?" Doreen asks.

"Looks like it!" I nod as I go to lift the vase.

"It's alright, you can leave them there until your shift's over," Doreen says. "This Eli guy seems like a real keeper."

"Yeah, I guess maybe he is," I say, and I pull my phone out of my pocket. "If you'll excuse me, I'll be just a minute."

"Take your time," Doreen replies with a smirk as Nala and her begin to talk amongst each other, and I head out toward the hallway overlooking the pond outside.

I'm nervous, but I decide to call him. I want to thank him for the flowers, and if we are ever going to be more than just chat and coffee friends—which, it seems like it's headed that way—I need to stop being so scared.

I let it ring a few times, and I go to hang up, thinking he's busy, only to hear a click on the other line.

"Hello?" Eli says, and I can't help but grin from ear to ear.

CHAPTER NINE

"Hey!" I say sweetly, my cheeks blooming a bright red, which I can see in my faint reflection in the glass of the window. "I got your flowers."

"You did?"

"Sure did," I say as I find myself pacing the hall like a teenager, all aglow, messing with a loose lock of hair.

"Do you like them?"

"They're beautiful, Eli," I reply. "I love them."

"I'm glad," Eli replied. "They're your favorite, right?"

"They sure are," I say as I beam brightly. This seems like a dream. Me, seeing a guy who is handsome and sends me flowers? Somebody pinch me. Joseph would never. Not unless he was trying to make amends of some sort.

"Guess my brain's still good for something," Eli jokes. "Darla, I want to ask you something."

"Sure, what's up?" I ask, feeling a bit jittery.

"I don't want to sound too forward but... is it weird that I miss you?" Eli asks, and my heart zooms through my rib cage and into my throat. Things seem to be moving so fast.

It feels like being on The Zipper at the state fair, the ride with the cages that flip and turn as you go around in a circle up high in the air. You don't know which way you're going to flip or turn... but all you know is the ride is fun. And I certainly don't want to hop off.

It's mighty dangerous but thrilling.

"Not at all," I reply. "I miss you too."

"Listen, I know we are supposed to have a date on Valentine's, but... I want to see you sooner," Eli says, and I can't believe my ears.

"Really? When?"

"Well, actually, I was hoping you'd have some time tonight," Eli says. "I want to take you to that nice country bar I was telling you about. Do you like to dance?"

"Well, depends on what kind of dancing," I reply, anxiously curling a piece of hair around my finger. Loving to dance and being able to dance are two very different things. And if I'm going to be completely honest, I have two left feet.

"Line dancing," Eli says, and I breathe a little sigh of relief.

"Well shoot, I haven't done that in years," I reply. *I can probably swing line dancing,* I think to myself. *I mean, it's just following along with the crowd. Though the last time I'd done it was... I don't know... when Sparrow was a baby?*

"Me either," Eli says with a bit of what sounds like a nervous chuckle. "So, want to go out tonight? We can do something different on Valentine's Day."

"That sounds lovely," I say, barely able to contain the squeal of happiness that threatens to escape my throat.

"Meet me at Moonshine and Music downtown when you get out," Eli says. "I'll shoot a text with the address your way."

"Alright, well, I'll get out, get dressed, and meet you there," I say as I realize Doreen and Nala are standing at the end of the hallway, gawking at me with big ol' grins on their faces. *Little eavesdroppers!* "I hate to cut this short, but I've got to get back to work."

"Alright," Eli says. "Well, I'll see you soon!"

"See you soon," I repeat back, and when I hang up, I can't help but twirl in the hall.

"Ooh, she's got it bad," Doreen teases.

"For sure she does," Nala says with a chuckle as I look over at them and smile.

"Stop it you two," I say with a giggle as I head back into the ward and quickly finish up my food. But I know they're right. Eli is wonderful and I'm falling hard and fast. . . it's as scary as it is invigorating.

There's one thing I can say for sure though. Even though I'm excited and terrified all at once, it really is an amazing feeling. I feel alive for the first time in a long time, and I can't wait to see where it all ends up.

Chapter Ten

Skylar White
Clean Romance

DARLA

I don't think I've ever gotten ready as quickly in my life as I have on this FaceTime call with Sparrow, frantically trying to figure out an outfit to wear to go line dancing. Eventually, between the two of us, we settle on one of my more western looking outfits, complete with a signature fringe.

It wasn't perfect, but at least it's something I could actually dance in—which most of my pin up dresses made impossible. I even completed the look by digging out my matching white cowboy hat and boots. I had to give those oldies—but goodies—a little TLC, wiping the dust off curved edges and pointed toes, but they looked great atop my blown-out curls and long legs.

Even though my outfit has me feeling somewhat confident, I admittedly feel a little out of place as I walk into Moonshine and Music. As my eyes glance around the bar, looking for Eli, they stop short as I become mesmerized by a huge group of people line dancing together in tandem.

They're so synchronized, in fact, you could have almost mistaken them for parts of a well-oiled machine. The last time I'd gone line dancing, it had been with Joseph, and there is something about that fact that adds to the anxious feeling growing in my chest.

I should go, I think to myself. However, as I heave a sigh and try to figure out how I'm going to explain to Eli why I'm canceling, I feel a tap on my shoulder.

"Well, hey good lookin'," a voice calls out from behind me, and I spin around to come face to face with Eli. As soon as I see him, my worries start to melt away, too stunned to have any thoughts in my brain other than ones about him.

Eli's dressed to the nines, wearing a fancy cowboy hat paired with a tight fitting, black button up shirt embroidered in blue at the top. It makes his beautiful tan skin glow, and the color of his eyes pop. Those jeans of his, also snug, are accentuated by a huge belt buckle—a longhorn steer head engraved into the steel, and the rim lined with turquoise.

"You're looking mighty fine yourself," I reply, and he beams at me big and bright, his teeth white and gleaming. "Hope you weren't waiting on me long."

"Actually, I was worried I was late," I fib, his voice slowly smoothing out all the apprehensions I came in with.

"Nope, right on time," Eli insists as he gently places his hand gently on my back. "Let's find a seat." "Shouldn't we alert the bar or a hostess?" I ask. "Nah, their waiters and waitresses are top notch," Eli replies. "They'll notice us."

I try my best to hide that I'm blushing as his hand glides across the back of my shoulders, a touch that truly sweeps me off my feet as he leads me to a cushioned wooden booth. Just like Eli said, a waitress comes to us with menus in no time.

It was typical Texan bar fodder—chicken wings, frito pie, steak, ribs, and stuff like that—all of it sounded delicious. I settle on some steak, even though I wanted the chicken wings, afraid I'd look like a barbarian eating them in front of Eli.

The food is amazing regardless, and so is the company. I could listen to Eli talk about literally anything for hours, his deep, rich voice one of the most calming and gorgeous sounds I've ever heard.

"So, would you like to dance?" Eli asks as he finishes his food, and immediately, my heart starts to race.

"Oh, um, I'm not sure if that's a good idea," I say.

"What do you mean?"

"I don't know how much I remember about line dancing to be honest," I reply.

"That's just silly," Eli replies. "Line dancing is about having fun. Come on, I can teach you what you don't know."

I sit for a second and think about it, the memories of Joseph and I dancing with one another seeping into my mind. *No,* I think to myself. *I'm not going to let him continue to ruin things for me. This is my time. My life. And it's too short to worry about what happened before or even about looking silly.*

I want to have fun.

"Alright," I reply with a nod, and I'm surprised when I stand up and Eli grabs my hand in his, our fingers intertwining as he leads me to the dance floor. I can't help but grin ear to ear, my cheeks ablaze as he takes me over to the side and away from everyone else.

"Trying to hide me?" I joke.

"Not at all," he says with a smile. "I just want you all to myself."

"Is that so?" I flirt back.

"Oh! you hear that?" Eli asks, and I hear Brooks and Dunn come on.

"Oh gosh, "Boot Scootin' Boogie!"

"Mm-hmm!" Eli says with a smile. "This is perfect! Alright then, you ready?"

"Ready as I'll ever be," I say, and with his hand still in mine he begins to guide me through the moves.

"So, it's right twice, left twice," Eli says as he clicks the heels of his boots on the ground.

"Right twice, left twice," I say quietly to myself as I do the same.

"Okay, now, right, left, right," Eli says, and I replicate it. "Good! Now, do a little hitch with your foot and turn."

"Like this?" I ask, kicking my foot up and crossing it over my other so I can turn.

"Yep! Just like that!" Eli replies, beaming brightly. "Now, do you know how to do the grapevine?"

"Do I!" I say as I do the steps, and he laughs.

"Good! Then clap and go the other way." As I do it, he lets go and comes in front of me to do it with me. "Now we're going to do a little rocking step with the little lasso move here," he says, and as he does it I can't help but giggle.

"What? Did I do something funny?" he asks.

"Oh no, I'm just having so much fun," I say.

"Me too," he replies as he continues to teach me the dance. "Alright then, you ready to give it a spin with me?" he asks.

"Yeah! Let's do it!" I say, and then the both of us start dancing, giggling all the while. I surprise myself, not only that I got it down so fast, but how fun it was.

I truly miss doing stuff like this, just going out and having a blast. Or maybe what I really miss is having this sort of connection to someone. Either way, the two of us continue to dance throughout the night, and he teaches me more moves.

"Okay, so, it's like this?" I ask and Eli shakes his head and laughs as he comes up behind me, surprising me when he gently grabs my arms.

"No, no, like this," he says as he guides my body, and I glance up at him just as his eyes flicker down to mine.

"Is this better?" I ask breathlessly, my face turning a bit more toward his.

"Yeah, like that," he replies quietly, and his face slowly begins to gravitate toward mine.

Oh my, this is it! He's going to kiss me! I think to myself. But then I hear a familiar laugh from across the room, and my face breaks away from Eli's, turning toward the sound. It's so loud I jump a little, and when I look over to the bar, I can't believe my eyes.

"You've got to be kidding me," I whisper.

"Pardon?" Eli asks.

"It's. . . it's nothing," I insist.

"It's definitely something," Eli says.

"My ex, he's. . . he's at the bar," I say, feeling a bit of anger crop up before it is quickly replaced by fear. The last words he said to me ring in my ears. "We should go," I say as I let go of Eli and make a b-line for the door, hoping Jospeh won't notice.

"Hey now, Darla! Wait a minute," Eli calls after me, but I'm moving far too fast, and he doesn't catch up to me until we get outside.

"I'm sorry. . . but we've got to go," I say.

"No, we don't," Eli insists. "So what if he's here?"

"You don't understand, Eli. He's awful," I say as my lip starts to quiver and tears begin to creep up in the corners of my eyes.

"What do you mean?"

"He's stalking me," I say. "At least I think so? I don't know, but he's constantly stopping at my house. The last time he was there I told him to leave me alone and he told me I'd regret it. . . and now he's here."

"Shoot. . . It's alright, darlin'," Eli says as he pulls me in close to him and holds me. I can feel my heartbeat begin to slow. "I'm not going to let anybody hurt you."

"Really?" I ask.

"Mm-hmm," Eli replies, his jaw tightening a pinch. "Point him out to me."

"Oh no, you don't have to get involved—"

"Darla, I care about you," Eli says, "and even if I didn't know you, I couldn't allow a woman to be terrorized by some jerk. So, point him out through the window, and I'll take care of it."

***

"There, sitting at the bar with those other three guys at the end, talking to them," Darla says, and as I squint through the glass, I'm shocked to see Mitch sitting there with them. He's leaned up against the wall and laughing with the other two.

She's got to be telling the truth about him being in there, I think to myself. *I mean, Mitch already admitted he's friends with the guy. But I'm sure he doesn't realize that he's been following Darla around.*

"Why don't you go on and wait in your car, and I'll come back in a minute, alright?" I say.

"Eli. . . don't," Darla says. "I'm not sure what he's capable of right now. He's acting. . . off."

"Don't you worry about me, I promise I can handle myself," I insist as I walk her to her car and then head back into Moonshine and Music.

"Which one of you two is Joseph?" I ask as I walk right up to the bar. One of the guys raises his eyebrows.

"That'd be me," he replies. "Who's asking?"

"Me, that's who," I reply as I feel the heat of anger crawl up my neck. "What kind of a man can't take "leave me alone" for an answer?"

"Excuse me?" Joseph replies, looking confused. But I'm sure it's all a charade.

"You being here when Darla and I are on our date after you keep showing up at her house," I snap. "That's what I'm talking about."

"Look man, I don't know what you're talking about," Joseph says. "I think you have me confused for someone else. I don't even know a Darla."

"Now, I know you're not going to sit here and lie to my face—"

"Hey, hey, hey, alright," Mitch says with a grunt as he gets up. "Excuse us, gentlemen."

Mitch guides me away from the bar, and he has an irritated look on his face. "Eli! What in the blue blazes are you doing?"

"Your friend is stalking Darla," I reply angrily. "I can't allow that."

"Oh, come on, Eli," Mitch says.

"He's already showing up to her house and threatening her," I insist.

"Says who?" Mitch asks.

"Darla," I reply.

"Man, I told you, she's crazy," Mitch says with a groan. "It's just a coincidence. He didn't even say anything about her or know that she was here 'til you said something."

"I don't think she is"," I reply. "Maybe you're just too close to him to see it, but he's obviously scaring the crap out of her."

"Or maybe you're too infatuated with her to see her for who she really is," Mitch snips back, and I heave a heavy sigh.

"No, I don't think so," I reply. "It's just too much of a coincidence for him to be here. Especially after what he said to her."

"And what was that?" Mitch asks.

"That if she turned him away, she'd regret it," I say, and Mitch shakes his head and groans.

"He could have said that out of anger," Mitch agrees finally. "I could see that."

"So, let me go over there and set the guy straight!"

"Eli, calm down," Mitch says. "Listen, there's no need to start a fight. I'll talk to him for you."

"Really?" I ask.

"It's better than making a scene at the bar, isn't it?" Mitch replies, and I have to admit, he's probably right—even if I do want to punch him in his ugly little pointed nose and teach him a lesson.

"I suppose," I say. "But make sure he knows that if he doesn't leave Darla alone, next time I won't just let you handle it."

"Ten-four good buddy," Mitch says as he pats my shoulder. "Now, go find her and figure out how to salvage the night, alright?"

"Yeah, you know what, I think I will," I say with a nod. "Thanks."

"No problem," Mitch says as he tips his hat. "We are basically kin now, I got to have your back," he says and heads back to the bar, returning to his seat next to Joseph.

Confident that Mitch has it handled, I head back outside and find Darla still sitting in her car. She looks terrified, and she scrambles out of the car and begins to look me over as soon as I get to her.

"Are you okay?"

"Right as rain," I say. "My ranch hand, Mitch, he's in there. He's actually talking to him right now."

"Oh boy," Darla says, sounding a bit panicked.

"It's okay, we got your back, Darla," I reply.

"I really appreciate it," Darla says with a sniffle as she wipes gently at her eyes. "Thank you for sticking up for me."

"Of course," I reply, but her face is still affixed in a frown. "You know. . . why don't we take this date somewhere else."

"Like where?" she asks.

"Do you like bowling?"

"Actually, I do," she says with a nod as her smile returns to her face, warming my heart.

"Well then, I know a place if you want to hop in my truck," I say, and she nods as she grabs my hand, squeezing it tightly as I lead her to it. As we drive, one of my hands in hers, I feel this sense of exhilaration I haven't felt in a long time. I really am falling hard for her, and I'd keep doing anything to see her smile.

**

After the hiccup at Moonshine and Music, I'm surprised that he would want to continue the date at all. Another man may have ended the night after all the drama, but not Eli. He's a different breed. A real man.

When we walk into the bowling alley, it's honestly a lot nicer than I expected. And since it was later in the night, the whole place was lit up with black lights, and anything close-by glowed neon everywhere you looked.

"Reminds me of when I was a kid and did that galaxy glow bowling stuff when I was younger," I say.

"Some fun times," Eli says with a nod. "Let's make some new memories." We bowl, and it's neck and neck the whole night, him winning a game, and me winning another.

"This is it, Eli, the last round," I say as I pick up another ball.

"Yeah, well, this time I'm not going to let you win," Eli says with a wink. "But do your best."

I head up to the lane, a neon pink bowling ball hooked into my fingers. The smooth backside of it is held by the palm of my other hand, cool to the touch. *Come on Darla, you got this!*

I let it loose, tossing the ball down the alley, crossing my fingers as I watch it zoom right down the middle of the lane. "Yes! That's it! Come on!"

The ball reaches the end of the lane and plunges into the pins, causing an explosion of sound as the glossy ball sends pins flying with a resounding clatter. I hold my breath as one pin twirls a bit, appearing to be holding on for dear life, until finally it falls to the floor.

"Yes! I win!" I squeal with delight as I turn around and Eli claps.

"Well shoot! Ya got me," he says with a laugh as he comes over. Without thinking, I excitedly jump into his arms.

"Did you see that?"

"I did, I did," Eli says with a chuckle. "Man, you're a good bowler. I guess I should have picked mini golf," he jokes.

"Hmm, maybe next time?" I ask.

"Maybe," Eli says as he releases me and holds out his arm instead; I take it in mine. We go and return our bowling shoes, head out to the parking lot, hop back into his truck, and head back to the bar so I can get my car.

Again, his hand slips into mine as we drive, and I can't believe how perfect he is. The night may not have been smooth or perfect, but it ended well. And besides, having his hand back in mine just feels... good. It feels right.

"Well, here we are," Eli says as he puts his truck in park. Both of us get out of the car and head over to mine, and though I'm elated about the night in general, I'm sad that it's ending.

"Thank you, Eli, for showing me such a lovely time," I say.

"The pleasure was all mine, Darla," Eli says, as he opens my door for me. "So, Valentine's, we can meet at my place?"

"Oh, um," I say as I sit down in the driver's seat, turning redder by the second.

"Oh! No! Not like that!" he says, looking completely embarrassed. "Not that I don't like you or want you in that way—"

"It's okay," I say with a laugh, trying to help relieve his frazzled mind. "What were you thinking?"

"Some horse riding in the morning," Eli says. "I have a mare that is very lovable, and I think you'd like her very much."

"That would be amazing!" I say excitedly as I stick my key into the ignition. "What time should I be there?"

"About ten or so sound alright?" Eli asks.

"Sure thing!" I say with a smile. "Well then, I'll see you in a couple days."

"Sounds good," Eli says. "Take care driving home," he says as he goes to walk away and stops in his tracks. "Matter of fact, text me when you get there so I know that you're safe."

"Okay," I agree with a nod, and I've swelled up with this weird little sense of happiness about it. He cares about me, that's for sure, and it feels good. "See you later!"

"Night!" he calls back as I turn my key, but it doesn't turn over. It just clicks.

"Oh no..." I groan as I try again, only to hear it click three times and then nothing.

"What's going on?" Eli says as he pops his head in the window, catching me off guard and nearly causing me to scream bloody murder as I put my hand to my chest.

"I'm really not sure, it won't start," I say.

"It's not turning over?"

"Not at all," I sigh. "I guess I'll have to call Sparrow."

"It's getting pretty late," Eli says. "Why don't you just let me take you back home? No need to wake up your kin when I'm right here."

"You sure? I really don't want to be an inconvenience," I say, feeling a bit embarrassed.

"It's no big deal," Eli says. "Come on, let's get you home."

I'm thankful for the ride, and as a bonus, I get to talk to him longer. The two us of sing along to the radio with the windows down, the wind whipping through our hair as we go.

I can't help but frown a bit as we finally turn up my driveway and he parks his big old Ford in front of my house.

"Well, this is me," I say. "Thank you so much again for such a wonderful evening."

"I'm glad you had as much fun as I did," he says as he squeezes my hand, and our eyes meet. I feel this intense desire to lean over and plant a kiss on him, the same feeling I'd felt when we'd been dancing at the bar. But, instead of giving in, I push it down and press a kiss to his cheek instead, leaving a red print on his skin, not wanting to seem like I was too easy or something.

"I'll see you on Valentine's then?"

"Definitely," he says as I get out of the truck, waving to him as I walk to the door, saddened as I watch him pull away. I never expected to be falling so hard and so fast for another man, but here I am, doing just that.

It's frightening and exciting all at once, but the fear is getting kicked to the wayside. All I can think about is when I'll see him next.

Chapter Eleven

ELI

I'm not even sure if I've slept at all when the alarm goes off on my nightstand, but if I didn't, I'm too amped up to even notice.

"Mornin' Mel," I say as I sit up. As I look at her photo, I feel a twinge of guilt crop up for the first time. "I know this is probably weird for the both of us, but I think you'd like her," I say before I get up and head to the bathroom to get ready for the day.

It's been mere days since I last saw Darla, but to me it feels like far longer than that. In fact, since I last saw her, the days have seemed to drag on. The feeling of her ruby red lips lingering on my cheek sticks in my memories.

"Hey, you almost done in there?" Mitch knocks just as I'm finishing up combing my hair.

"Yeah, I'm good," I say as I step out into the hallway.

"Well, holy smokes, you look even more dapper than usual," Mitch says.

"Thanks," I say with a smile. "Hopefully Darla likes it as much as you."

"Ah, you're still seeing her?" Mitch asks, his smile smoothing into a straight line. "After all that drama she caused at the bar, I figured maybe you'd have gotten the hint."

"Nope," I say with a shrug. "She's coming here for Valentine's Day, actually."

"Here?" Mitch asks, seeming to be surprised.

"Well, yeah, she likes horses," I reply. "I figured it would be a nice treat for her."

"I really think you're making a big mistake here," Mitch insists. "I'm telling you, Joseph says—"

"Respectfully, I'm not really interested in what he has to say," I reply and gently push past him, heading for the kitchen.

"I'd say he knows her better than either of us," Mitch continues as we both reach the kitchen. I open up the fridge and grab the milk, shredded cheese, and some eggs.

"I know you mean well, but I told you already, I like her," I say. "Just because we have a difference in opinion about her, it doesn't mean it has to be a thing."

"She ruined Joe's life," Mitch insists.

"Don't do this," I sigh as I get out the big mixing bowl and begin to crack eggs into the bowl.

"I'm telling you that you don't know the whole story!"

"And I'm telling you that Joe isn't the nice guy you seem to think he is," I say as I turn to him, and I can see the anger on his face. "He's a coward and a cheater."

"I—"

"I think what we need to do is just put this to bed," I say. "I'm not going to change my mind on this. Besides, cheaters are awful people, and someone who would threaten a woman isn't too great either."

"Eli—"

"Mitch, I told ya I don't got time for this!" I snap, and Mitch gets really quiet for a moment, a bit of red creeping onto his face.

Boy, he's getting way more upset about this than I imagined he would. It's so weird. I get being loyal to your friends and all, but he won't even listen to me or consider what I'm saying.

"I'm sorry," Mitch says as he draws in a deep breath through his nose, slowly releasing it.

"It's okay," I reply as I continue to break eggs into the metal bowl. "I just want to make breakfast, make sure I'm all ready for when she gets here, and have a good day."

"Right," Mitch says quietly, looking down at the floor as he nods his head. "I, uh, I gotta use the bathroom before I get to chorin'."

"You aren't going to eat?" I ask.

"I'm not hungry," Mitch says quietly. "I need to get my work done so I can cut out early, got a date of my own."

"Oh! Well, alright," I say, not liking the tension hanging in the air between us. "Hey, when you go out there, would you mind mucking the horse stalls?"

"Sure," Mitch says, his smile obviously forced as he heads back to the bathroom. *His reaction to this whole situation seems like overkill*, I think to myself. *Hopefully this date of his will leave him in a better mood...*

**

I'm buzzing with excitement as I weave through the backroads of Thistleberry on my way to Eli's for our early morning Valentine's date. Lucky for me, Doreen talked to one of the overnight gals, and she's covering my shift today so I could make it. Otherwise, it would have been a bust—which would've been truly heartbreaking.

Ever since he'd driven me home, our texts have become more and more frequent. We text whenever we can, from when I get up until I go to bed, which is really nice. But the longer I'm away from him, the more I feel myself longing to be near him again.

I have to admit, however, that I'm also really excited about getting back in the saddle. Even though it won't be the same without my beautiful mare, it's something I have really been looking forward to. Besides seeing Eli of course. In fact, it's really sweet of him to even offer to do this. I mean, trusting someone with your animals is a big deal, I certainly wouldn't ever have let just anyone ride my Laney, that's for sure.

Red dust kicks up all around me as I turn up the lane to his house and the pavement disappears. I roll up my windows, not wanting to ruin my makeup before I get there, and squint through the billowing clouds of crimson to look for the sign he said I'd see at the end of the road.

Finally, I find it—the sign with a beautiful Texas rose pattern carved into it—hanging over an open gate and drive on through. I pass by a small, dark building, but I keep going, looking for a white house.

When I get there, it's bigger than I expected, surrounded by a dirt dusted white fence and a porch that wraps around the whole front of the place. It feels like being back at my daddy's old ranch, so I feel oddly at home as I open the gate and walk through.

My confidence from before wanes a bit as I go to knock on the front door, but I choose to ignore it. I deserve to be happy, I deserve to move forward, and I'm not going to let Joseph, or anyone else stop me. The past is the past, and I'm leaving it there.

I give the door a hearty knock, and after a few moments, it slowly cracks open. I expect to see Eli standing there, but instead I see a very young man in traditional western yoke, paired with a matching cowboy hat and some well-worn jeans.

"Oh, um, hi," I say with a little wave.

"Morning," the young man says. "You must be Darla."

"And you must be... Zack," I reply, remembering that Eli said that Zack had blue eyes and Noah has brown ones. The only real difference between the two.

"Guilty as charged," Zack says with a chuckle. "We've heard a lot about you," he says as he opens the door wider, and I can see Noah peering at me from the large kitchen table.

"Good things I hope," I reply.

"Well, all except for that pie thing," Zack says with a chuckle.

"Zack, don't tease Dad's woman," Noah calls out.

"Oh, come on," Zack replies. "I'm sure she can take it if she's with Dad."

"He's alright, Noah," I say with a smile. "Thank you though."

"Are you boys torturing, Darla?" I hear Eli say from somewhere deeper inside the house, and then finally there he is. He's dressed in another, more traditional, buckskin, long sleeved shirt with fringe across the chest, and tight jeans.

"Nah, just making conversation is all," Zack insists, and Eli pushes past him and comes out on the porch. "Remember you two, I need you to work double time to make up for me today."

"Aye, aye, Captain," Noah says. "Nice to meet you, Darla!"

"Yeah, nice to finally meet you," Zack chimes in.

"Likewise," I reply as Eli closes the door behind him.

"They seem like nice boys," I say to Eli, who is looking down at me, our bodies close and his soft blue eyes nearly turning me into a puddle as I return his gaze.

"They can be," Eli says with a chuckle. "You look gorgeous," he says as he lightly brushes a stray strand of hair behind my ear.

"T-thank you," I stutter, holding my breath, wondering if he's about to kiss me. A part of me wishes he would. I'm tingling from head to toe in anticipation.

"Oh, um, I got you these," Eli says as he pulls something from behind his back, and lo and behold, it's a bouquet of tiger lilies and a box of chocolates.

"Oh, Eli! They're so lovely!"

"Nothing could ever be as lovely as you," Eli says, and I feel my heart swell in my chest. "Let me go put these in water really quick and set this candy down so we can go about our business," he says, breaking the tension. At least for the moment.

"Alright," I say as I stand on the porch and wait, and a few minutes later, he's back out with a singular stray lily.

"What's that for?" I ask as he gently snaps the stem short.

"For your hair," Eli replies as he gently places it behind my ear. "I thought you might like it."

"I do!" I say with a smile as I catch a peek of my reflection in the window.

"You ready to go check out the place?" Eli asks as he slips his hand gently into mine.

"Sounds like a plan," I reply, and he leads me out behind the picket fence and toward a long, dark red barn.

"I'm glad you could make it here today," he says as we walk across the rocky ground. "Especially with the way your car petered out the other night."

"Oh! Yeah, that's the strangest thing," I say. "Daniel looked at it for me, and I guess someone messed with my battery cables."

"Messed with them how?" Eli asks.

"Well, he thinks that someone was trying to steal it and panicked," I reply.

"Really? Even though you were parked that close to the bar?"

"I guess so," I say with a shrug. "From what he told me, they put the battery cables back on wrong. Backward he said, like they were in a hurry."

"Holy smokes," Eli says. "You're lucky the thing refused to turn over."

"Why do you say that?"

"Well, because if it had started, it could have quickly overheated and blown up."

"Really?" I ask, genuinely surprised.

"Yeah," Eli says quietly as we reach the barn, and I can tell that he seems a bit out of sorts, though I can't quite put my finger on why. Instead of opening the door, he pauses for a moment. "Joe's not bothering you anymore, is he?"

"No, he's left me alone," I say as his face softens again and he opens the door.

"Well good, I'd hate to have to knock him down a few pegs," he says as we walk into the humongous barn. "This is where we keep all the horses, I think we are up to fourteen now."

"Oh wow," I say as I look around. "It's so roomy."

"Yes, well, I like my horses to be comfortable," he says. "Gives them ample room to lay down and such."

"Makes sense," I say with a smile. I hear rustling from one of the open stables before a man with a purple bandana on his face comes out with a bucket.

"Oh, um, this is Mitch," Eli says. "He's my friend and ranch hand."

CHAPTER ELEVEN

The man stands there silently, bucket dangling in his hands as he almost seems to glare at me.

"Nice to meet you, Mitch," I say, but instead of saying hello back, all he does is wave before he turns tail and briskly walks off.

Strange, I think to myself. *Most cowboys are really friendly and talkative. Maybe he's just shy.*

"Anyways, you ready to meet Lilah?" Eli asks, and I push the quiet man out of my head.

"Born ready," I say excitedly as he steers me to a pen holding a beautiful brown mare with a white streak sliding up its nose, peaking in a cute little point at its forehead.

"Oh my, she's so beautiful!" I gasp as I gingerly reach my hand in and pet her before he brings her out and gets her all ready to go. He then helps me onto her back, and hands me the reigns, the tanned leather feeling so good in my hands.

"I'm glad you like her," Eli says. "She's very gentle," he says as he pets her neck. "Been a while since she's been ridden."

"Been a while since I've rode," I say with a giggle. "So, I guess we have that in common," I say as I watch him lead out a lovely black stallion.

"Seems like the two of you will be fast friends," Eli replies. "This is Tango. I've had him the longest."

"He's precious," I say as Eli gets Tango ready and hops on.

"You ready to go?" he asks, and I feel a bit nervous as I grip the reigns tightly.

"Definitely," I say.

"Well then, let's ride."

He takes off, and I flick the reigns and take off after him, out the open back door and into a beautiful, green, grassy field. The property is huge, two or three times the size of my father's, and Eli and I explore it all. All the while, there's a smile on my face as the wind whips through my hair.

"I got someplace to show you," he says after about an hour of riding around, and he races up a hill. It's a little bit steep, but Lilah seems to know the way and isn't bothered at all by it. So, we continue to chase after him until we get to the top.

"Look at this view!" I say, the gorgeous hills and valleys like something out of a Kincade painting.

"Isn't it?" Eli says. "I thought you might like it."

"I certainly do," I say as I take a deep breath in, the scent of dirt and grass filling my nose. "It's lovely."

"I own all the way out to that fence there," Eli says. "And then to that mountain face right there."

"Oh wow, that's even bigger than I thought," I say.

"Yeah, well, I wanted to give us room to be self-sufficient," Eli says. "Back in the day this cost quite a pretty penny. But I got it done."

"Reminds me of home," I say out loud as the thought brews in my head again. "My father is a farmer and rancher all wrapped into one, or was, he's retired now. I miss it. I miss the animals too."

There's a lot pause of quiet, the only sound that of the breeze whistling through the tree branches. The day had been lovely, and here I was, making it awkward by being homesick.

"You know, I got something that you might want to see down in the pig barn," Eli says with a smile. "You interested?"

***

It's hard to pay attention to where I'm going as Darla and Lilah get a little lead on me, Darla all aglow as we continue our ride. She's ethereal, like an angel sent down from God, and everything about her is perfect. So, how could she be as bad as Mitch says she is?

We ride on out to the pig barn, our bodies so close as I put my hands on her hips to help her hop down, and she puts her hands on my shoulders. The desire to kiss her is sickeningly strong. But I decide against it.

Not yet. Not 'til I'm sure we are both ready.

"So, um, pigs," I manage to get out, and she snorts with laughter.

"You okay there, big shot?" she asks as she peers up at me.

"Yeah! Yes! I'm totally fine," I say, and it makes her laugh even harder.

"Okay, so what did you want to show me? Pigs, you said." Darla gently nudges me, and I realize I've just been standing there, admiring her beauty.

"Right," I reply. "Come inside with me."

I open the door and when she takes my hand in hers all on her own, I can't help but grin from ear to ear as I lead her to the pig pen with the piglets.

"Aw!" she squeals with delight. "Babies!"

"I thought you might take a liking to them," I say, glad that she's cheered up from earlier. Being homesick is no fun, and I didn't want our day to be ruined because of it. Nor did I ever want to see Darla sad.

"Can I play with them?" she asks.

"Well sure, though I don't know if they'll play or not," I say with a chuckle as she climbs right in and sits down in the hay. The piglets all scatter at first, squeaking and oinking. But, much to my surprise, she's able to coax a few her way and pet them. One in particular seems to fancy her, staying in her arms until it dozes off.

And this is supposed to be the toxic woman I should stay away from? I think to myself. *She couldn't hurt a fly.*

As I watch her with the babies, another thought flies through my mind, and I feel my jaw tense a bit. I'm concerned about that battery incident, and something inside me says she's being too relaxed about the whole thing. I mean, Joe was right there at the bar that night, and he'd already threatened her. What if he was the one that did that to her battery?

"Eli?" I hear Darla call out, one of the piglets still in her arms.

"Yes, dear?" I reply absentmindedly.

"You alright?" she asks as she cocks her head at me.

"Me? Oh yeah, no, I'm fine," I say. "Just admiring you."

"Is that so?" she asks as she scratches the belly of one of the piglets.

"You're like some sort of animal whisperer," I say.

"Well, I don't know about that." Darla laughs. "Though, I always wanted to be a veterinarian."

"Really?"

"Yeah, but I couldn't handle having to put animals down if I had to, you know?" Darla replies. "It's too sad for me."

"Don't you lose people at the hospital?" I ask.

"Well, yeah," Darla replies. "But that's only been a recent thing for me and trust me, I don't like it. Back home I was on labor and delivery, so death was rare. But when I transferred, there were no spots open in that department, ICU or ER was all they had. So, I picked ICU."

"That's rough," I reply, shaking my head. "I couldn't do what you do, Darla. You're a hometown hero."

"I wouldn't say that," Darla says. "I'm just doing my job. Helping people is something I have always been passionate about, you know? Everyone deserves to receive the best care and kindness they can while they're in the hospital and healing up. I'm only doing what's right."

When I thought I couldn't fall for her any more, her words touch my heart. *What a woman,* I think to myself as I smile, and she continues to play with the piglets.

Eventually, I crawl in too, but unlike her, the pigs want nothing to do with me, which cracks her up. And by the time we climb out of the pig pen, we are both covered in hay and mud, her jeans especially dirty.

"I guess we will have to name you pigpen now, instead of pie girl," I tease, and her giggle sends giggles up my spine as I help her up.

"You're dirty too!"

"Yeah, but I like picking on you," I say with a grin as she climbs through the bars and lets out a gasp when she loses her footing on the other side.

I dash forward and catch her, helping her back up when her eyes peer up at mine with such intensity I can feel myself catching on fire. She then slides her hand behind my neck, gently rubbing the nape of it as I pull her in closer, and our lips finally meet.

The kiss is nothing short of electrifying, and I can't help but lean into it, deepening the kiss as we stand there in the barn all alone. I feel like a man possessed as I linger even longer, until we both pull back breathlessly.

"I'm sorry if that was too forward," I say to her. But all she does is smile as she gets on her tip toes, kissing me again. I feel like my head is in the clouds, and if this is what I might feel for the rest of my life, this intense joy, then I don't want to come down.

However, the moment is spoiled when something clammers behind us. I let go to look, only to see that Mitch is standing there picking up the feed buckets he'd dropped and eyeing the two of us, bandana still across his mouth.

I wonder if he's getting sick, I think to myself. *Or maybe the stalls just smelled worse today...*

"I'm sorry if I've embarrassed you in front of your friend," Darla says, and my eyes flicker back to her, a worried look on her face.

"No, of course not," I say with a shake of my head. "How could I ever be embarrassed about someone seeing a pretty young thing like you on my arm?"

"I'm not that much younger than you!" Darla says with a snort, and we head out of the pig pens and back outside, where we spend the rest of the morning together.

We check out the cow barn, feed the chickens, and do some more riding until my watch goes off, and I feel the corners of my mouth tug into a frown. She's got to go get some sleep to cover an overnight shift, and I've got chirping to get done. But I truly don't want her to go.

We bring the horses back to the barn, and with every step toward the house, it feels like my legs are dragging. Anticipating her departure, and wanting to ask her to stay. But I know I can't. I go into the house and glumly retrieve her candy and flowers and bring them back out to her, trying my best to keep up the happy smile I've had on my face all day.

"I believe these were yours," I say as I hand them off to her.

"Thank you," she says, and I realize that she looks a little sad too.

"The pleasure is all mine," I say as I quickly grab her hand and kiss the top of it. "It's been a lovely day."

"It really has," she says. "I can't remember ever having a day so beautiful."

"Me either," I reply, and she gets up on her toes and gives me a kiss on the cheek.

"Sorry I couldn't take you out for dinner," I say.

"It's alright, I'm glad we could at least do all of this," she says. "Now I get to go home, shower, and nap before my overnight shift."

"That doesn't sound fun," I say.

"Eh, it's pretty quiet," she replies with a shrug. "Though, I will miss my texting buddy."

"Oh, your boyfriend's not going to be awake?" I tease.

"Is that what he is?" Darla asks, and the question hits me hard.

Is that what we are now? Girlfriend and boyfriend?

Am I even ready for this?

"Yeah," I say, pushing all my doubts away. I know how I feel about her, and I'm not going to let Mitch, or my past, get in the way of it. I haven't been this happy in a long, long time. And I'm going to lean into it. "That is, if she'll have him."

"She will," she says, a bit low and sultry, her fingers gently grasping at mine as she looks up at me with a big grin on her face.

"He's a lucky man," I joke, and she kisses me again, this time softly on the mouth, and I can hear my heartbeat in my ears.

"He sure is," she says with a wink.

"About dinner," I say. "Let me make it up to you."

"Make it up to me?" she asks.

"Well, yeah, Valentine's dinner," I say. "How about the day after tomorrow? That gives you time to rest and whatnot from your shift."

"Sure, though I do have to work, so it'll have to be late again."

"For you? I'd eat at one o' clock in the morning," I say as I walk her out to her car, hand in hand, feeling over the moon.

A girlfriend... I have a girlfriend.

"Should we meet somewhere?" Darla asks, and I shake my head, the battery situation still bothering me.

"I'll just pick you up at home or something," I say.

"You sure?" she asks.

"Yeah, it's no big deal," I say with a shrug as I open her car door for her. "Drive safe and have a good nap."

"You enjoy the rest of your day too, shug," Darla says as she kisses my cheek again before climbing into her car and shutting her door. I stand there as I watch her back out, cheesing like a fool as she waves to me, though I still feel a tug of disappointment as she pulls away.

What is this? I think to myself. *It's been so long since I've wanted someone other than the boys around.*

As I walk back into the house, I'm not sure how to feel about it. But by the time I have a seat in my recliner, I can't help feeling anything but happy. I'm alive again, and I have Darla to thank for rekindling that spark in my soul.

"You have a good time, Pops?" Zack asks, and I open my eyes as he sits down on the couch.

"Yes, actually," I say. "What'd you think?" I ask, worried that he might not like the situation at all. He's older now, but still. He really misses his mama, and it still shows in the way he acts.

"She's real pretty, and she seems nice," Zack replies.

"Does it bother you?" I ask.

"What do you mean?"

"Me dating Darla," I reply, and Zack clears his throat a little.

"At first, I didn't care for it," Zack says. "But then I saw the two of you today out there having fun. You were all aglow on top of Tango, the two of you laughing and carrying on. How could I be mad at that?"

"Dad?" I hear Noah yell from the door. "Dad? Zack? Are you in here?"

"Yep! We're in the living room," I say as I sit up a bit, and Zack comes flying into the den, a worried look on his face. "What's the problem?"

"I don't know what happened, but somehow the gate got loose," Zack says. "We got a bunch of cows spilling out into the yard and hills. I need your help."

Strange, I think to myself. *I checked and double checked that gate as Darla and I were running around, and Mitch has been working the barns all morning.*

"Don't worry," I say as I shake it off. It could've been a mischievous heffer that knocked something loose. "We'll get them back. Did you tell Mitch?"

"Actually, I'm not sure where he is," Noah says.

"Well, he can't be too far, unless he's left for his date already," I say with a groan as I get up out of my chair. "Let's get to work then, can't let them get too far or old man Willy next door is going to cuss me out again. Last time, they ate up his begonias."

Chapter Twelve

DARLA

Caked in mud and my heart as light as a feather, I nearly dance my way inside the house, riding the high of the day. The horse ride, the piglets, that kiss! And Eli asking us to be official in the most perfect way? It was the best way to end the day, and to make my heart sing in a way it hasn't in years—in a way it never has.

Sure, I had loved Joseph, but even with him, the feelings hadn't been this intense. This was a whole new world for me, full of this almost magical, fairytale-like rush of feelings, and I'm on cloud nine.

I peel off my dirty clothes and take a shower, and as I suds up my hair, all I can think about is him. His ruggedly handsome face, the way his lips felt against mine—soft yet manly as he kissed me hard in the barn, not caring who saw.

It feels good to be that wanted.

Darned good.

I get dressed in my pajamas, humming to myself as I twirl around, closing my handy dandy blackout curtains to get ready for a nap. Though, I'm not sure how I can with how worked up I am. Instead, I decide that maybe I should eat some lunch first before I try to lay down—a full belly might help.

Maybe if I drink some chocolate milk with it, I think to myself. *Always worked when I was pregnant with Sparrow.*

I make myself some eggs, bacon, a few sausage links, and some frozen waffles, sighing as I sit down at the empty kitchen table. It feels good to be with Eli, but when he's not around, I've started to feel lonelier than ever. It's not the greatest, but I suppose that all good things come at a price, and Eli is certainly a good thing, so I'm willing to deal. At least, for now.

My new doorbell rings, singing a sweet little southern melody as it jingles throughout the house. *Who could that be?* I wonder as I take another bite of my waffle before getting up to answer it. Before I can make it to the door, I'm hit by this sickening dread, and I freeze in place.

I just got back from Eli's, and now the doorbell's ringing? I think to myself as I quietly creep toward the door, sneakily sliding an umbrella out of the little metal bin by the door as I brace myself for a slew of vitriol. . . or worse. But as I swing the door open, umbrella hidden behind my back, I breathe a sigh of relief when I see it's Sparrow and Jade.

"Hey, Mom! You okay?" Sparrow asks.

"Oh! Hello there!" I say as I slip the umbrella back into place. "Oh yes, I'm fine, just eating brunch."

"You're sweating," she says as she points to my forehead and Jade claps and squeals with delight. I put my fingers to it, and sure enough, a well-developed bead clings to my fingers.

"I'm not sweating, I'm glistening," I joke as I let them in and close the door behind them.

"Must've missed a bit when I blow dried my hair after I got home."

"Oh yeah, your date!" Sparrow says as she lumbers in with Jade and the diaper bag in tow, letting it slide off her shoulder and fall to the floor. She then puts Jade down before rummaging through the bulging bag, pulling out a semi crinkled envelope.

"Happy Valentine's Day!" she says as she hands it to me. I carefully open it and inside is a lovely card from everyone, and a little folded up heart with Jade's handprint on it.

"Oh my gosh, that's so sweet!" I say as I scurry off to the kitchen and put Jade's little valentine on the fridge, and the card on the table.

"Well, I figured you deserved something nice from your favorite little one," Sparrow says as Jade crawled over to the little toy chest I had for her. Sparrow sits down at the kitchen table next to the bouquet of wild lilies Eli had sent home with me. "So, how'd that date go?"

"It was amazing! He's so sweet! We went out riding on his ranch, and I got to play with the piglets. He has such a beautiful property," I gush, but I hold back a bit, feeling like I have to be careful of what I say.

I know Sparrow is angry at her father, but I would never try to pit her against him, and I didn't want to offend her by giving her the full scoop.

"Now, I know it couldn't have been just that with the way you were gushing about him when Daniel and I showed up to help with your car," Sparrow sighs. Perceptive little bird saw right through me.

"You're right, it was a little bit more than that," I say, a smile I can't contain slowly slipping across my face.

"Well, spill the tea," Sparrow says.

"We kissed," I said excitedly, and Sparrow's eyes went wide.

"Really?"

"Yep! And he asked me to be his girlfriend!" I reply and I'm pleasantly relieved when Sparrow grins.

"I'm so proud of you! Look at you over here glowing!" she says. "You look like a whole new woman."

"Oh gosh, Sparrow, stop," I say as I try not to blush.

"It's true," Sparrow says. "Ever since you started seeing Eli, there's this radiance about you. It's something I haven't noticed in you in a long time."

"You know what? I definitely feel it," I say with a sigh as I sit down to finish my breakfast. "I feel ten years younger at least!"

"You deserve it, Mama," Sparrow says as she lays a hand on top of mine and gives it a little squeeze.

"You're right," I reply. "I really do, don't I?"

"Mm-hmm!"

"I'm just glad I found a good one on there," I say as I bite a piece of bacon. "There's some real wild ones on that dating app."

"What do you mean?" Sparrow asks, and I just shake my head, not even wanting to get into it.

"I'll tell you when you're older," I tease as I finish my breakfast, play with Jade on the floor until they leave, and then crawl into bed. Finally able to sleep, visions of Eli and I together dance across the back of my eyelids.

***

"Hyah!" I yell as I rush around the back of the herd of cattle with Mitch and the boys, Tango speeding around like he was a young buck still, not showing any signs of aging. Me on the other hand, my hips are sore from riding all day with Darla, and now having to round the cows up—who thankfully had stayed more or less all together—had me aching for a nice hot bath and some time planted in front of the television.

"Did we get 'em all?" I yell to Zack and Noah, who are heading up the back.

"Yeah, I think so," Zack calls out as I meet back up with Mitch at the front.

"Sheesh, that was rough," I say to Mitch, but he's eerily quiet, and no longer wearing his bandana on his face. He appears to be deep in thought. "Still not sure how this happened."

"I guess we'll have to check everything when we get back after we get these guys and gals up, hmm?" he replies quietly.

"Yeah," I say, trying to gauge where Mitch's head is at. The tone in his voice is level, but it also seems full of an emotion I can't quite peg. It feels like the calm before a storm, and I don't much like it.

"Look like the date went well," he says finally after about five minutes of our silent ride to take the cows back.

"It sure did," I say. "She's a wonderful woman."

"Agree to disagree, but you know what, I'm glad you're happy," Mitch replies, his face affixed in a scowl for a moment before leveling out.

"You seem angry at me," I say.

"Less angry, more disappointed," Mitch replies. "I'm trying to protect you, Eli. But you just won't let me."

"I think the one you need to be protecting yourself from is that Joe guy," I say, trying to figure out how to ease into the possibility that Joe was trying to hurt Darla, but unsure how to without upsetting him further.

"Joe is a good man," Mitch insists, shaking his head. "It's too bad you didn't meet him first or seen the things I've seen."

Seen the things he's seen? What things? I think to myself. Darla only just moved here, and there he is again, making claims about things he shouldn't know.

"Well, I hate to break it to ya, Mitch, but I believe that man has it out for Darla," I say, and Mitch looks over at me, his eyes seeming like two hollow pits. There's just nothing there.

"Is that so?" Mitch asks.

"I think he tried to hurt Darla," I say, and Mitch stops short, the cattle beginning to walk around him. So, I stop just behind him. "The night he and I had words at the bar, after I took off with her like you said, we came back, and her car wouldn't start."

"So?"

"Her son in law looked it over and someone messed with her battery, put the cables on the terminals backward," I reply. "It could have blown right up."

"That's not possible," Mitch says as he shakes his head.

"Is it not possible, or you just don't want it to be?" I ask him and I see his jaw move around as if he's fighting back anger.

"Joseph was with me all night," Mitch says. "I saw him get in his car and leave."

"So, you're saying he doesn't have the capability to come back and mess with it?" I say.

"How do you know Darla didn't do it to herself?" Mitch asks. "Who got there first?"

"She did," I said. "But—"

"But what?" Mitch growls. "You don't think that wench is capable of popping her hood and rearranging some cables?"

"Watch your tone when you speak about my girl," I say angrily.

"Ah, so she's your girl now," Mitch says quietly.

"That's right, she is," I reply. "And your ol' buddy Joe needs to stay away." Mitch gets quiet again, and the silence is deafening, even as the massive sea of cows moves past us.

"Well, if that's the case," Mitch says before he pushes me as hard as he can off Tango, and my head slams into the ground below.

What. . . what just happened? I think to myself, dazed and trying to get to my feet, shaking my head as the ringing in my ears lessens until it's more of a dull roar.

"What the heck, Mitch?" I say, and I just barely make it to my feet before I get trampled by oncoming cows, using Tango's rump to steady myself.

"It's really too bad you couldn't take the hint, cowboy," he says, and he leans over Tango with something in his hand. "Now I got to take you out of the equation."

CHAPTER TWELVE

Before I can even register what he's said, Tango rears up, whinnying in pain as he begins to act wild, and I try my best to calm him down. I fail miserably, feeling the slam of one of his hooves smashing into my skull, and as I lay on the ground and watch Tango take off, everything fades to black.

Chapter Thirteen

DARLA

I'm still riding the emotions of earlier into the night as I get into work, settling in at the nurse's station and looking over my list of patients for the night. I'm still grateful that LuAnne was able to switch with me, but there's something about nights on the ICU that always makes me nervous. The silence is unsettling and a little bit eerie, not knowing which one of my patients wouldn't make it through the night.

"Got a new one for ya," an ER nurse says as she pulls someone through, his face all bandaged and taped up.

"No one called me to tell me anything," I say.

"Well, emergencies aren't planned are they," the ER nurse snips, and I hold my tongue. I know the ER is stressful, but there was no need for attitude!

"I suppose not," I say instead, forcing a smile as the woman thrusts the clipboard from her hands into mine.

"There ya go," she says. "What room's open, so I can get him set up?"

"Right there is fine," I say, motioning to the empty room directly in front of me. "Thanks," she says as she rolls her eyes, ruffling my feathers further. I decide to ignore her and look through the chart.

CHAPTER THIRTEEN

Elijah Garcia, 70 years of age, severe brain injury. . . emergency brain surgery. . . Jesus, this guy's in rough shape.

I look up from the clipboard to see the nurse still working on hooking him up. Getting the IVs plugged up, sticking the EKG modules on his chest, and blood pressure cuffing his free arm. That eerie feeling comes flooding back again and riles up my stomach.

I can't wait to get the heck out of this ward.

The hours go by, and whenever I'm not helping a patient, I'm nearly falling asleep at the desk. Already, one has almost died on us, an open-heart surgery survivor, and another woke up and tried to pull their breathing tube out and had to be sedated.

I don't know how people keep this up all the time, I think to myself. Just me and another nurse covering the sizeable ward all by ourselves really isn't enough. And I'm not even sure if it's legal, even on overnights.

"Hey, Darla," Jennifer says, the other nurse on duty, as she walks back to the desk. "Look alive, we have another one coming up."

"Another?" I say sleepily. "Jeez, tonight is just full of surprises, isn't it?"

"Never a dull moment," she replies as she looks at the clipboard.

"We got a name?" I ask.

"Eli," she replies, and I shift uncomfortably in my seat.

"Eli, huh?"

"Yep," she replies. "Brain injury. He's in surgery right now since this Elijah guy needed help first. But this one's not looking too hot either."

"What's the last name?" I ask, my curiosity piqued. I'm very aware there are other people in the world named Eli, but I just want to be sure.

"Garcia," she says, and my eyes go wide.

"Garcia?" I repeat, my voice cracking.

"Yeah, why?"

"What's his age?" I ask.

"Looks to be. . . fifty-four," she says, and suddenly I feel like the whole world around me has ceased to exist. My vision gets blurry, and my hearing is muffled. I can tell that Jennifer is talking to me, I can even feel her hand on my shoulder as she tries to shake me out of my daze. "What's the address?" I ask.

"Pardon?"

"Does it list the patient's address?" I ask frantically.

"No, Darla, you know that's not on here," Jennifer says as I snap back to reality.

"Next of kin? Anything?"

Jennifer looks at me like I'm a complete lunatic, or maybe it's just a look of worry. Either way, I need to know who, if anyone, is on that list.

"Four boys," she says. "Jeffrey, Robert, Noah, and Zack."

My blood runs cold, and everything left in my stomach comes up as I rush to the garbage can and heave into it. "This cannot be happening!" I cry, my own voice echoing in my ears as Jennifer rubs my back.

"Darla, are you alright?"

"I need to go down there," I say as I wipe the tears from my eyes, so thick and stinging so bad I can hardly see. "I need to go see them."

"Oh my gosh, do you know them?" Jennifer asks as I manage to stand up.

"Eli's my boyfriend," I told her.

"Oh my. . . Go Darla!" Jennifer says as she waves for me to go.

"I'm sorry," I say as I run as fast as my legs will carry me to the elevator, pressing the button rapidly until it finally opens. It feels like ages before the door finally closes, and I head on down to the ground floor, streaking through the halls and trying to find the operating rooms.

"Hey, hey, woah," a voice says as I skid to a halt, and in front of me is the last person I want to see right now or ever again. Joseph.

He's coming out of the cafeteria, and on a quick glance I notice there's blood on his jeans.

"What are you doing here?" I ask.

"A friend got hurt, he's in the ER," Joseph sighs. "Bar fight."

"Well, I'm sorry about your friend, but I need you to move out of my way," I say, trying to stay calm.

"You can't stop to chat?" Joseph asks. "I'm real worried about him."

"I ain't got time for you and your dumb drinking buddies," I say as I try to push past but he won't let me.

"Slow down, what is going on?" Joseph asks.

"Nothing that concerns you," I say as I try again, but he blocks me.

"Now, don't be so sassy, Darla," Joseph says. "That's no way to treat a concerned friend of a patient in your hospital, now, is it?"

"Seriously Joe, now is not the time," I say.

"When is it the time when it comes to you?" Joseph asks.

"As far as you're concerned? Never," I say as I finally bob and weave enough to get past him. "My own friend is in trouble."

"Wait," Joseph says as he nearly flies around to get in front of me again. "Listen, I'm sorry about the other day."

"Joe—"

"I'm sorry I got so heated, I just miss you so much," he says, "I love you Darla, I miss what we had. What we could still have."

"We have nothing anymore Joseph, don't you see that?" I say. "Throughout our whole marriage, I did everything I could to make you happy. I helped build our home, I gave you two beautiful babies and all the love I could give even with your busy schedule. But then you decided to burn it all to the ground."

"Come on, Darla," Joseph says as he puts his hands on my shoulders. "We can fix it, there's still time."

"No, we can't, Joe!" I snap as I shake my head. "No amount of apologizing or gifts will ever, ever fix what you've done," I growl through gritted teeth.

"You are my wife," Joe snaps, anger finally bleeding to the surface as his gentle hold on my arms becomes a painful grasp.

"We are divorced, Joe," I say, not wincing or showing even a bit of fear. I refuse to let him think he has one over on me. "Now either you move out of my way, or I'll have you escorted out. Find another sucker."

He looks at me for a moment, appearing to be dumbfounded by my words, so I rip his hands off me and continue to run down the corridor. He continues calling out for me and I keep ignoring him as I focus on the sign that says, "operation waiting room" on the wall, and I follow the arrow.

When I enter the room, I see Zack, Noah, and another man who I assume to be Jeffrey in there, the two twins sitting together with their heads hung, and the other brother pacing back and forth behind them.

"Zack? Noah?" I call out, and both their heads pop up, and I can see their eyes are red and puffy.

"Darla!" Zack says as I run up to him and instinctively wrap my arms around him. "What are you doing here?"

"I work here," I say. "I just happened to be covering the night shift tonight, and the other nurse read off the chart. . . I didn't want it to be true."

"It's awful," Zack cries, burrowing his face into my shoulder as Noah stands up and rubs his back lightly.

"It's going to be okay man," Noah says. "Dad wouldn't want us to be a mess like this."

"I don't think Dad's going to know," Jeffrey says as he walks over to us.

"You must be, Jeff," I say.

"And you must be the new girlfriend," he says with a sigh. "Nice to meet you, wish it was under better circumstances."

"Likewise," I reply. "What happened?"

"The cows got out and Mitch, Zack, and I were rounding the cattle up. Next thing we know, Dad falls off his horse and Tango kicks him."

"Tango? Really?" I ask. "He seemed so well behaved."

"We think he got stung by something," Zack says. "There's a little wound on his shoulder."

"Where's Mitch? Did he see what happened?" I ask.

"He's here somewhere," Noah replies. "He was right there actually. Said they were talking and then everything got crazy."

That seems fishy, I think to myself for a moment, but it's a fleeting thought, my hands shaking as I let go of Zack and sit down, the adrenaline coursing through my veins tapping out. I sit with them all night, and it's not until the sun starts peeking through the windows that someone comes out from the OR to speak with us.

"He made it through the operation," the nurse says. "But to be honest, with how hard that kick hit, and how much blood we had to release from the hematoma, we aren't sure what the damage will be over time."

"What are you saying?" Jeffrey asks curtly. "You mean to tell me that you don't know if he will be okay?"

"Brain injuries are touchy," I say, trying my best even at my worst to try to calm Jeffrey down. "They won't know until he wakes up and sees how he does."

"Jesus," Jeffrey groans angrily, muttering to himself as he sits back down.

"Thank you for letting us know," I say as the nurse gives me a little nod.

"We will see if he rouses from the surgery on his own, which could take a few hours," she says. "Either way, he will be brought up to the ICU then. You're welcome to stay here or head home to gather up some things for him."

"I've got to get some headache pills in me," Jeffrey says as he rubs his temples. "Are you guys heading up to the house to grab stuff for him?"

"Yeah, I guess Mitch went home and got his toiletries together at least," Zack says as he looks at his phone. "Thanks for sitting with us, Darla."

"Of course," I say as my lip quivers, the mask I've been wearing to try to keep calm starting to slip.

"We will keep you updated, okay?" Zack says as he hands me his phone and has me put my number in.

"Thank you," I say tearfully as the three boys head out, and my legs, fawn like and wobbly make me have to sit down again.

Of course, I meet the man of my dreams and he's now in critical condition, I think to myself as I finally let it all out, crying loudly in the big, lonely room. Unsure of what to do with myself other than put my hands together in prayer, I hope for a miracle.

Chapter Fourteen

Skylar White
Clean Romance

DARLA

I had offered to stay and wait for Eli to get on the ward so the nurse on call in my place could go home, but she had refused. So, I'd spent the whole day—though I was supposed to be asleep—either lying in bed crying or pacing the floors of my house. I spent hours waiting for Zack to text me, to say anything.

But the text never came.

I was still scheduled to work a mid-shift, and I did my best to hold myself together, hoping beyond hope that when I got there that Eli would be alright. Eventually, when I get to the nurse's desk, all eyes are on me.

Just as expected, the gossip mill always turns no matter where you work, and the day crew whispers as I shuffle through the charts. I look for Eli's and Eli's alone.

My eyes flutter up for a moment and I notice that the old man from last night isn't in his room either. To get the hens of the roost to stop murmuring, I decide to ask about him.

"Where's Elijah?"

"He's out for an MRI right now," one of the girls say as I continue to thumb through the charts, still not finding the one man I'm looking for.

"Where is Eli Garcia's chart?" I ask calmly, my eyes wandering over to the other nurses.

"You mean, Elijah," one says.

"No, I mean, Eli Garcia," I say. "Fifty-four, head trauma and brain surgery."

"Doesn't ring any bells," another one says, and I turn around to look at the whiteboard on the wall.

No Eli Garcia.

"Move out of my way, please," I say to the nurse in front of our floor's computer, and she eyes me suspiciously as I sit down and my fingers fly across the keyboard. I enter my username and password, and begin searching the ER, OR, and ICU database for records of an Eli Garcia. *Just as I thought, ER released him to OR... but where did he go after? Did he need a transfer to a bigger hospital?*

I clamp my hand over my mouth as I read the words, muffling a loud, painful scream that sends the whole ward into a panic.

Eli Garcia, Male, 54, deceased. Made it through the operation with success, but then seized downstairs in the recovery room, and passed away. Patient has been moved to the morgue and placed under the care of Doctor John P. Fisher, hospital pathologist.

"No," I say out loud as I nearly fall out of my chair. "No, no, no!"

"Darla?" I hear Doreen call out, but I am balled up on the floor at this point, sobbing uncontrollably.

"He's gone," I say. "Eli is gone."

"Quit gawking at her and help me get her off the floor you morons!" Doreen yells at what I assume is the other nurses, and with their help, I'm eventually taken off the cold tile floor, and seated in a chair.

"Darla," Doreen says quietly. "I think we should call Sparrow and let you go home."

"No... I can't... I have bills," I say.

"Paid," Doreen says. "One way or another. But you need to go home. I can't have you here like this. It's not good for you or our patients."

"Okay," I say shakily as I take out my phone and find it without word from the boys. Weeping inconsolably, I call Sparrow and attempt to explain what's happening, all of it feeling like a nightmare that God could have ripped such a beautiful light out of this life so soon. A light that I needed, one that was now extinguished, along with any hope I had left that life wouldn't always be so painful.

***

Beep.

Beep.

Beep.

"Will you..." I start to say, wanting someone to shut the beeping up, every beep making me wince in pain as my eyes slowly opened. But my mouth feels like someone's poured a gallon of sand in there and left it, my tongue like cracked, desert mud, and so I can't seem to get the words out.

Everything hurts. Head to toe. And as I try to move, I realize that I can't. Not easily at least. I hear snoring to my side, and slowly look over to see someone sitting in the chair next to me. *Who is that?* I think to myself as I look at his curly hair. *My son? Zack...* asleep and loosely holding my hand.

What's going on? I think to myself as I try to speak again, but my head pounds and I feel nauseous. "Ugh," I manage to get out as I move my hand up toward my head, only to see a blood pressure cuff attached to my arm. *Am I in the hospital?* I think to myself. *What the heck happened?*

"Z-Zack," I croak out, and he stirs a little. So, I squeeze the hand in his grip as hard as I can and try again. "Zack!"

"Huh? Wha—?" Zack murmurs as he finally begins to wake up, In the dark of the room, I can see his eyes open wide as he looks at me.

"Oh my gosh, you're awake!" Zack exclaims. "Don't move, I'll get the doctor!"

"Wait," I whisper, but he doesn't hear me, flying out the door and leaving me alone with my thoughts. *I'm in the hospital. Got it. But why? What happened to me? I feel like I lived through an earthquake.*

I sit there and think, but nothing comes to me, and I'm becoming increasingly frustrated. *What do I know? I know my name is... Eli. Yeah. That sounds right. And I have... four kids, boys. Jeffrey, Robert, Zack, and Noah.*

Where do I live? I ask myself, and pause to think, even though it's making my head hurt worse. *Up on the ranch... in a white house that Mel and I bought together.*

Mel! I think to myself, but then, like a bad movie, my brain shows me the accident. The car had been torn to bits. *She's gone. She's been gone. I don't know how long, but she's left us.* Other than that, I don't remember anything.

CHAPTER FOURTEEN

"Mr. Garcia!" a man in a white coat says cheerfully as he strolls into the room, the words "Doctor Jacob Trachner, MD" embroidered above his breast pocket. "Nice to see that you're awake."

"Garcia? Is that my last name?" I ask, things still feeling fuzzy and out of place in my head. It's as if my mind was a bookshelf and someone has toppled it over, and now I am struggling to get everything back in order.

"Yes, that's our last name, Dad," Zack says, and I nod. I figure Zack would know best.

"You've been through a pretty serious accident, Eli," the doctor says. "So, I need you to make sure you stay still, at least for now."

"What happened?" I ask.

"You fell off your horse, and got kicked in the head," Doctor Trachner replies. "It's caused some bleeding in your brain and a part of your skull has been damaged."

"Is that why everything is so hard to remember?" I ask. "Is this normal?"

"Unfortunately, yes," Doctor Trachner replies. "It will take some time to know how extensive the damage is to your brain. But the fact that you're awake and alert is a great sign."

"Will I. . . be like this forever?" I ask, and the doctor sighs.

"We are unsure at this time," Doctor Trachner says. "But since you're awake, I would like to have you participate in a simple neurology test. I want to see what you can remember."

The doctor then asked me a slew of questions about my kids, my house, my wife. He also asked me who the president was at the time, which I couldn't remember.

"Thank you, I'll let you rest now," the doctor says when I've answered everything I could. "Remember, don't cause him any undue stress," he tells Zack before he walks out and leaves us alone.

"Want to watch some TV while we wait for Jeff and Noah?" Zack asks.

"Sure," I say. "Not like I'm going anywhere."

Zack gets me some water, and he helps me sip it with a straw before he puts on *Gunsmoke*, the two of us silent as we watch the magic of technicolor on a small, flat screen.

The silence lingers for a while as he sits there, feverishly texting someone on his phone. I'm not sure if he's afraid to talk to me, or if he's unsure of what to say or what not to say. So, I decide to poke at him and see what he knows. The doctor summarized what happened to me, but it isn't making sense in my head. I mean, why would a horse kick me?

"Zack," I say.

"Yeah, what's up, Dad?" Zack replies. "Do you need me to get you something? Want me to see if you can eat?"

"Maybe in a bit, but right now I need to ask you something," I say.

"Sure," he replies.

"Do you know what happened to me?" I ask.

"Not exactly," Zack says with a sigh. "You and Mitch were helping wrangle the herd that somehow escaped, we still aren't sure how. And then Tango reared up, knocked you off his back, and kicked you."

"Tango. . . yes I remember," I say. "He's young but he's a fine horse, not a mean or temperamental bone in that horse's body. That doesn't make sense."

"What do you mean by young?" Zack asks.

"Well, he's only a few years old," I reply, but I can immediately tell by the look on his face that I'm wrong.

"Dad, he's thirteen," Zack replies, looking a bit sad. "If he was a baby, I would be a tiny kid, right?" It takes me a second, but I realize Zack is right. He's a grown man, which means Tango would be an adult horse by now.

"Jesus. . ." I breathe, feeling a bit overwhelmed by the jumble in my brain.

"And what about Robert? Is he coming? You didn't mention him," I ask.

"No, he's still in California," Zack says, and though I don't remember it, I am sure he's right. Unlike the other boys, Robert was the wild one, and for him to head off to California makes sense to me. "Listen, the doctor said not to get you riled up," Zack replies. "I think we should talk about this later," he says as Jeffrey and Noah filter into the room.

"Boys!" I called out, trying to force a smile, but it stung. I put my finger to it, only to find a dab of blood there when I pulled it back to look. It's either chapped or cut, but I'm not sure which.

"Hey, Dad!" Noah replies cheerfully, but I can see Jeffrey hanging back, giving a little wave. He's always been sensitive, just like his mama was, and when he's upset you just know.

"Hey, can I talk to y'all in the hallway please?" Zack says, and the other two nod.

"We will be right back, I promise," Noah says as they go out into the hall, pulling up the door behind them. But not enough, because I can hear them talking fairly clearly. Save for a little hiccups here and there.

"Listen, I already talked to the doctor before about this, but we need to not force any memories and get him stressed out," Zack says.

"Well, what about Darla?" Noah asks in a lowered tone, and the name gives me pause. *Who's Darla? And why are they suddenly whispering?* I ask myself. When I try to remember, all I get in return is a headache.

"Well, she works here on the ward, I imagine she'll understand what he's going through," Zack replies. "I'll text her about this later so it's not a surprise. We got to be careful with him right now, Doc says he's fragile. He's got partial amnesia."

"Better he doesn't know," another voice I don't recognize says, and a man in a black shirt and jeans follows after it, wearing a cowboy hat and looking at me glumly.

I wonder what he meant by that...

"Hey there, boss man," he says.

"Boss man?" I ask, confused by the nickname.

"Oh no," Zack says as he rushes in after the man.

"It's alright," I insist, holding my hand up to hush him. "I'm sorry, but who are you?"

The man makes a face, and then smiles. "I'm Mitch, your ranch hand and good friend. I live at your house with Zack and Noah."

Thinking about it for a moment, I say, "Your face looks sort of familiar... you moved here from Amarillo, right?"

"Yes sir," Mitch says with a nod.

"I don't remember moving you in, but I remember you coming in for your interview," I think out loud. "I dressed nice; the boys picked on me for it."

"Yes! I've been working for you near two months now," he says. "Don't worry, I been making sure all the animals are fed and taken care of while you been gone, with the boys' help."

"I appreciate that," I reply.

"Look Mitch I'm glad ya came but they want us to keep it low key for now," Zack says, and Mitch makes another face.

"Alright, well, try to take 'er easy," Mitch says, his smile growing into a grin. "I got to check on the animals anyhow. That one cow's fixin' to give birth any day now."

"Thank you, Mitch," I say, and he tips his hat to me before he walks out and the rest of my boys come back in.

They stay with me for quite a while, even though it's the middle of the night, and though I'm supposed to be sleeping, I find that I can't. *Why is everyone being so weird about everything? And why can't I know about Darla? And why does Mitch not seem to like her?*

So many questions, but no answers.

I guess it'll have to wait.

***

My eyes feel like I've been socked in both eyelids as I drive myself to work. Doreen had given me two days off, and she even said that if I needed more time to let her know. But I don't have any choice but to go in. The bills aren't going to pay themselves with me sitting at home, crying myself stupid.

"You alright?" LuAnne asks, who apparently had come in to work in case I didn't show.

"Never been better," I fib as I sit down in one of the chairs at the long desk and begin to look over the charts.

Well, I see Elijah is still kicking, I think to myself, and my eyes flicker from the page and up toward his room. Suddenly, I'm hit with a wave of shock as I see someone familiar standing in Elijah's room.

Noah.

What is he doing in there? I wonder, feeling this mixture of confusion and concern. *My gosh, is this old man the kids' grandfather or something? Eli never said what his parents' names were.*

I can't deal with this right now, I think to myself, seeing that my name is still listed on Elijah's chart as his nurse. *They haven't even texted me to let me know, those poor boys. I don't think I can handle facing them right now. I don't want to cause another scene either, especially at work. I can't lose this job.*

"LuAnne?"

"Yeah?"

"You mind switching with me? For this patient?" I ask, showing her the clipboard.

"Um, sure, I guess," LuAnne replies meekly as I erase my name and put hers at the top. I go to the board and do the same with one of hers, taking responsibility for one of her patients.

I spend most of the time fluttering around, taking care of as many patient's problems as possible just so I can avoid Elijah, the boys, and his room. All the while, my brain was whirring and wondering what exactly happened with them and if they were okay.

By the time I finally got the nerve to go to Elijah's room, it was near the end of my shift, and no one but Elijah was in the dark room, most likely asleep. So instead, I clocked out, hopped in my car, grabbed dinner on the way home and took it to my room.

As soon as I walk through the door, I'm hit by the fragrance of lilies. And when I see that huge vase that he'd had delivered to the hospital, I begin crying all over again.

I feel so angry and sad all at once as I curl up in bed and eat my food. How could I have been so close to happiness only to have it ripped away from me all over again? The world. . . this life. . . it's too cruel.

Chapter Fifteen

Skylar White
Clean Romance

Darla

"Thank you for coming in on such short notice," Doreen says as I walk into the ICU. She called me in to work the night shift since I have the day off tomorrow and LuAnne called in sick. Honestly, I need the money, so I didn't make a fuss.

"It's really no problem," I say. "I like to help out, it helps me feel useful."

"Yes, well, after what you've been through, I have to say that you're one of the strongest women I know," Doreen says. "I sure as heck wouldn't be here."

"Thank you," I reply, and clam right up. I know it's meant as a compliment, but I can't help but think that I'm not that strong at all. If anything, I just feel shattered inside, like I've been broken for so long that it's become second nature—maybe even before losing Joseph. For me, if I don't keep going, I might stop existing completely.

"Alright, well I got to get home now," Doreen says. "Jacqueline will be in later to help with the shift. Until then, you are the head woman in charge."

"What time does she come in?"

"Well, it's about ten now, so probably around midnight," Doreen says as she looks down at her phone, then slides it into her pocket. "Just a warning, she isn't feeling so hot either, but she's decided to push through it."

That's not too bad, I think to myself. *It could be worse. I could be all by myself for the entire night, which I've seen happen to some of the other girls since I've started here.*

Not that I can blame Doreen's leadership. She's doing her best. But the hospital just isn't willing or able to give us the people we need. Which can be a real pain, especially when it's really busy.

"Here's your charts," Doreen says as she hands me a stack of clipboards. "See you later!"

I immediately begin looking through the charts to see if Elijah is still here. Sure enough, after a few moments of searching, there he is, and I'm listed as his nurse for the evening.

Just like I had before, I avoid Elijah's room like the plague, not wanting to run into any of the boys. It makes me feel like a complete and utter coward that I can't even face them, but the wound is so fresh I can't even talk about it to Sparrow. I'm sure all they need is some blubbering woman they hardly know hanging around and making things worse.

"Hey, Darla," Jacqueline calls out to me from the nurse's station.

"Yes?"

"Have you checked on Elijah yet this hour? We need some vitals from him, and I did it last time since you were busy."

"S-Sure, I can do that," I reply, feigning cheerfulness. But immediately my palms start to sweat as I move toward his room, and I feel a little heady.

It's just a checkup, I tell myself as I enter his room. *It's the middle of the night, he's not going to be much for conversation anyway.* Still, I can feel my anxiety roar to a fever pitch as I press the blood pressure button and get out the thermometer, standing over him in the dark.

"Evenin'," the old man says quietly, his crackly, half-awake voice nearly making me jump out of my skin.

"O-oh! Sorry if I woke you," I say, as I fumble with the thermometer in my fingers, holding it in front of his mouth. "I just need your vitals."

"It's alright," he mumbles as he gingerly takes it, opens his mouth wide, and then shuts his lips over the probe. After a few moments, the thermometer beeps, and I feel a sense of relief washing over me. *It's almost over,* I tell myself. *Now, all I have to do is get out of here and write these down. Guess that wasn't so bad after all.*

"Wait," the old man says, his voice clearing up a bit. It was still a tinge grainy, but oddly enough, not old sounding at all. At least, it wasn't how someone his age would sound like in my head.

I stop in place, my hands shaking. *Of course, it couldn't be that easy,* I think to myself as I turn back around, forcing a smile. "What can I help you with, Mr. Garcia?"

"Would you mind getting me a glass of water?" he asks, and I'm dumbstruck by how much he sounds like Eli. *It's my brain trying to deal with my grief,* I tell myself, and I shake it off, grab his pitcher, and fill a paper cup to the brim.

"Thank you kindly," he replies, and I'm hit once more with that weird sense of déjà vu. *Obviously, he's related to Eli since the boys have been around to see him—but maybe they just sound alike.* "Would you mind helping me drink this?"

"Of course," I say, as I shove my emotions down and help him drink, placing the straw in the cup and holding it for him while he gently sucks through the straw. For a man that had just come out of a coma, especially at his age, he seems to be doing well. But his head is still wrapped up like a mummy.

"Thank you so much," he says as he finishes, and I set the cup back on his side tray.

"It's no problem," I reply with a sigh. "If you need anything else, just press your bell."

The rest of my shift was fairly quiet, which wouldn't be such a problem if my brain wasn't on fire after hearing that voice.

I'm riddled with guilt. The boys are the real victims here, having lost their father. I'd only known him a short time, and I'm devastated. But Eli had raised them, and I can only imagine how they feel. I mean, I haven't even given them my condolences... It just wasn't right.

Finally, 7 a.m. rolls around, and once I pass the shift to the morning crew, I dart for my car. Those boys are without a mom or a dad now, and if it were my kids, I'd want somebody to check in on them and make sure they're okay.

I drive out to the grocery store and grab a pie, some flowers, and a condolence card, and head up to the house. It was the least I felt I could do, given the circumstances. As I go, my fingers are white knuckled on the steering wheel the whole way. I wonder what I'm even going to say. *What can I say? Nothing is going to make this any better. But maybe I can ease their pain just a little somehow.*

I get to the house and I knock on the door, standing there nervously with pie and flowers in hand. I see a head pop through the curtain and look at me, but then it promptly disappears. For a moment, I fear that they don't want to talk to me. That maybe I should just walk away. But then, slowly, the door creaks open, and there stands Noah, rubbing one of his eyes sleepily.

"Oh, hello there, Ms. Darla," Noah says, seeming surprised to see me.

"Hey there," I reply, holding out the pie. "I'm sorry I didn't come sooner. I'm so sorry for your loss. Your father was a good man."

"Wait. . . what are you talking about?" Noah asks.

"Eli," I reply, feeling a bit flustered by his lack of emotion. "I heard of his passing through the other nurses," I fib, not wanting to admit that I used my credentials and the computer at work to search for answers.

"Well, they told you wrong," Noah says. "He isn't dead. He's actually been awake and alert, he's just having some memory issues."

"What?" I gasp, nearly dropping the pie as I sit down on the little bench by the door.

"Zack! Get me some water." I hear him say as a wave of dizziness washes over me. The two boys hand me a cool glass of water, and I shakingly bring it to my lips to sip.

"But the computer at work said that he died," I reply, feeling very confused. "It said that he had a seizure and didn't make it."

"Well, that's not what happened at all," Zack insists. "He's been awake for a day or so."

"On the ICU ward?" I ask, still feeling fifty shades of stupefied.

"Yep," Noah replies.

"But I just worked last night and he's not in any of the charts," I say, and Noah's eyebrows furrow.

"Something's fishy here," Noah says, his brow furrowed. "Why don't we go over to that hospital with you and try to figure it out."

"I agree," Zack says with a nod. "Let's get you sorted and then roll out. You can ride with me, Ms. Darla."

Chapter Sixteen

DARLA

"See, there he is," Noah says, stopping in front of Elijah Garcia's room.

"That's Elijah's room," I say as I walk over to the nurse's station, still in disbelief as I pull Elijah's chart and cover everything up but the name and age, not wanting to get fired for a HIPAA violation. "See?"

"Woah," Zack replies. "Well, I'll be dipped, she's right."

"Obviously I can't show you the computer records, but I saw them," I say with tears in my eyes. "They said he was dead and I just. . ."

"Sheesh, this is a nightmare," Zack says as he hugs me from the side. "I'm sorry, I should have texted you. Things just got so crazy!"

"It's okay, I just figured you guys were going through enough," I reply. "I didn't want to be a bother."

"Yeah, well, now we have to figure out what in the blue blazes is going on here," Noah says. "Something about this whole situation has been weird to me from the beginning."

"What do you mean?" I ask.

"Noah please don't start with your conspiracy theories right now," Zack groans. "Let's just figure out why dad is dead on paper."

Conspiracy theories? I think to myself. *I wonder what Zack means by that.*

CHAPTER SIXTEEN

"Alright," Noah sighs, and while my curiosity is piqued as to what they're talking about, I decide to leave it alone. "So, what do we do?"

"Is his doctor also Doctor Trachner?" I ask.

"Yeah," Zack replies.

"Wait here," I say as I walk through the ward, searching for him and finding him in another patient's room. "Excuse me? Doctor Trachner?" I say, peeking into the room.

"Oh! Darla! What are you doing here?" he asks. "Weren't you on the overnight shift last night?"

"Yes, well, I need to speak with you about something important," I say.

"Alright, well I'll be there in a moment," Doctor Trachner says before he turns back to his patient, and I slink back to the hallway to wait. When he comes back, he passes right by me, but I'm hot on his tail. "Doctor Trachner!"

"Ah, there you are!" Doctor Trachner replies, stopping to turn to me. "What seems to be the trouble?"

"Elijah Garcia is not Elijah Garcia," I say, and Doctor Trachner raises his eyebrow at me.

"I don't follow. . ."

"Someone messed with the charts," I reply. "That's not Elijah Garcia, that's Eli Garcia."

"That's not possible, Darla," he says as he shakes his head. "Listen, I've heard that you lost someone—"

"That's just it, Doc," Zack calls out from behind me, "she didn't."

"Their father is Eli Garcia, not Elijah," I say. "And Eli—my boyfriend—is in that bed. I checked the computer, and the record claims Eli is dead. But I can assure you with one hundred percent certainty that he's not."

"You're sure?" the doctor asks, his voice cracking.

"Elijah was in his seventies," I say. "Does he sound like a seventy-year-old to you?"

"Oh boy," he says with a sigh. "I was wondering what a seventy-year-old man was doing taking care of horses. . ."

"And you never thought to check on it?" I ask.

"Well, no, because I trust the staff. . . and you can't see half his face because of the bandages," he says. "I thought Eli was just his nickname. It's what I heard that one friend of his call him. . . This is bad."

"Very. Not only is this not Elijah, but Elijah's family also has no idea that he's dead," I reply, and Doctor Trachner deflates immediately, a look of terror on his face.

"I've got to go fix this," he says. "Or at least try... Thank you, Darla!" Doctor Trachner says, and before I can say anything else, he starts jogging toward his office.

"Thank you for setting things straight," Zack says.

"It's really no problem," I say as I stand there, wringing my hands. "I'm just really glad he's okay."

"He's doing as well as he can right now," Noah says. "I hope they recheck him after all of this, make sure there's nothing else going on in his brain, that his meds are right..."

"I'm sure they will," I say, trying to reassure them. But after witnessing this major faux pas, I'm not really sure how much I trust the hospital. Or at least, the computer system. But even if the computer system had messed up, how did no one catch this mistake?

"Would you like to see him?" Zack asks.

"That would be lovely," I say as I try not to cry, feeling immensely relieved that the nightmare is over.

"There may be a problem..." Noah says.

"Why's that?" I ask.

"Well... remember when I said he doesn't remember stuff?" Noah begins, and immediately, it hits me.

"He doesn't remember me, does he?" I ask. "That's why when I helped him drink last night, he didn't say anything to me about it."

"Unfortunately, it's true," Zack confirms, and I feel a new sense of grief. "Did you still want to try?"

I stood there for a moment, trying to shuffle through the new sense of loss I'm feeling. To be in love with someone and to watch them die was already a cruel fate. But to love someone and be forgotten is still painful, just a different kind.

At least this way, there's a chance we can make it work, I think to myself, trying to stay positive. *Maybe he will remember me again. Or, if need be, I can get him to fall for me again. Hopefully, if the new Eli and I click. Anything is possible.*

"Yes, I do," I say.

"Well alright then, let's take you in."

CHAPTER SIXTEEN

***

Quiet whispers wake me up as Zack and Noah walk through the door, putting a smile on my face. Even though things are still a bit odd for me in the brain department, I hate being here in the hospital. However, the two of them visiting as much as possible almost makes it tolerable.

"Hey there!" I call out to them cheerfully, yawning loudly before blinking my eyes to try to get rid of the lingering haze. I then notice that there's someone lingering behind them, but much to my surprise, it's not Jeffrey.

It's a woman, but not just any woman. She's far different than anyone I recall seeing before. I mean, even with amnesia, there's no way I could forget someone who looks like *that*.

When she finally steps through the doorway, the morning light glimmers across her skin, making her look like an angel even though she's teary-eyed and in scrubs. She's got big, beautiful, doe-like brown eyes that are easy to get lost in. Her long lashes brush against her porcelain skin, which contrasts greatly with her vibrant, ruby red lips, but she makes it work to her advantage.

I feel a fluttering in my chest as she comes out from behind them and begins fussing with the flowers by the window, a bouquet of something in her own hands. She seems nervous, and frankly, for some reason, so am I. Who wouldn't be. . . in the same room as her?

"Hey, Dad," Zack says as the mystery woman continues to play with the get-well cards and flowers near the window. "We've brought a friend with us."

The woman turns toward me, and is now more composed, beaming big and bright.

"Hello, Eli," the woman says, and her voice is such a sultry, smooth tone that it gives me goosebumps.

"I'm sure I'm supposed to remember you," I say with a sigh. "But sadly, I don't."

"That's alright," she replies as her eyes open wider for a second. She scampers back to the window and places the lilies she brought into a vase. I stare at them for a moment as the morning sun gleams across their petals. There's something about them that's familiar.

"You know. . . I feel like I knew a girl who liked lilies," I say.

"Yeah, that's me," she replies with a nod, her eyes welling with tears all over again. I try to think hard, but still, nothing. "Lilies are my favorite."

I feel horrible, but the woman in front of me doesn't even register in the limited number of memories I now possess. It's a real shame. I hate that she seems so upset; I want to comfort her in some way, but I'm not really sure how.

"What's your name?" I ask, giving in to the fact that I'm completely stumped.

"I'm Darla," she says, and I begin to study her even more closely. So, this is the girl that everyone has been whispering about. . .

"You're gorgeous you know," I say, and I can see a blush blossoming on her cheeks as a smile pushes through the tears. "I've been told I'm pretty good looking myself, though you wouldn't know it what with me being half wrapped up like a mummy."

She laughs, and the very sound of it gives me butterflies in my stomach and fills me with this odd, happy feeling. After all the days of being stuck in the hospital and all the pain, it makes me feel human again, filling my AC-chilled bones with radiating warmth.

"Well, I can say with confidence that you certainly are, with or without the bandages," Darla says with a wink. "I just hope in time you'll remember me, or at least that we can become friends."

"I hope so too," I say as she offers me her hand to take, deciding to be bold and kiss it. "Because I cannot imagine a world where I could forget a pretty face like yours."

***

After visiting Eli for a few more minutes, I need a little bit of a break. Although it's nice to see him, and he's still the same charming Eli, it's hard to accept that all the memories we've made together have just evaporated into thin air. . . at least for him. I know it's not his fault. Accidents happen. But I'd be lying if I said that it doesn't pull at my heartstrings and bring on a new wave of hurt.

Either way, I'm not going to abandon him, that's for sure. No. I'm going to stick around and see what happens. However, there is something I do need to take care of—figuring out what exactly went wrong with the hospital records.

"Thank you for letting me see him," I say to Zack as he walks me out.

"No problem," Zack replies. "We are supposed to be a bit gentle with him, but you can visit whenever you want."

"Well, to be fair, he is my patient," I say with a snort. "I thought I was going insane last night when I heard his voice, but I didn't recognize it was him given the circumstances. Plus, it was really dark in there."

CHAPTER SIXTEEN

"Understandable," Zack says as his eyes flit away from me, and I turn to see Doctor Trachner walking through the hallway.

"Excuse me," I say as I pat Zack on the shoulder, "I've got a mystery to solve."

Before he can answer, I'm already long gone, stalking Doctor Trachner and pulling on his arm before he ducks back into his office.

"Hey!" he gasps as he twirls around and then puts a hand to his chest. "Oh, it's just you," he says, and I cannot help but notice the little bit of annoyance in his voice.

"Yeah, it's me," I say. "So, how's the detective work going on the case of the two Garcia's?"

"Well, from what I can tell, it was all just a big mistake," Doctor Tracher says quietly. "I'm sorry for the confusion and the stress that it's caused you."

"You're lucky nothing bad has happened to him and that he's been given the right meds and stuff," Noah growls from behind me, catching me off guard. "What if he'd been given the other guys' meds? He could have gotten hurt!"

That is strange, I think to myself as I listen to Doctor Trachner and Noah go back and forth, Doctor Trachner trying his best to fend off Noah's threats of a lawsuit the best he can. "Mr. Garcia, I'm really not sure what happened, but I don't think a lawsuit is in order." Doctor Trachner laughs nervously. "These kinds of things happen from time to time..."

Noah is right. If Elijah had died, and obviously Eli hadn't, but his identity was mixed up... how did they know to give him the correct meds? I think to myself. I wonder for a moment if I should ask the doctor about it, but I decide against it. Especially while Noah is tearing him a new one.

I'll do some snooping on my next shift, I think to myself. *It's obvious that Doctor Trachner seems to be more interested in covering his own butt than helping, that's for sure. He just wants to make it go away. But something here isn't right, and I'm determined to get to the bottom of it.*

Chapter Seventeen

Skylar White
Clean Romance

ELI

"How ya feeling today, Pops?" Jeffrey asks as he settles into the chair next to me.

"I'm doing okay I suppose," I reply, my mind still in the clouds from Darla's visit. "Doctor says we can take a look at how the incision is healing today, and hopefully I won't have to have these mummy bandages on anymore."

"Annoying, aren't they?" Jeffrey asks.

"Very," I say with a sigh. "But being in the hospital in general isn't exactly a party either."

"Amen to that," Jeffrey says as the door opens, and like she's read my mind, in comes Darla—the beautiful woman that's been running through my thoughts since we'd met. Well, met for the. . . well, I don't know how many times we've met honestly. But, since the first time that I can remember.

I'm excited to see her, to be honest. This time she's dressed in neon pink scrubs instead of the minty green ones I'd seen her in earlier, and the color seems to better suit her bubbly personality.

I remember hearing that she was a nurse, but I didn't expect to see her up here in the ICU. "You miss me or something?" I tease as she goes around and checks all the flowers like she did the other day.

CHAPTER SEVENTEEN

"You could say that," she says with a little giggle and a wink that pills my skin. "I'm actually here for work this time though."

"You're my nurse?"

"Yep!" Darla says with a grin. "I work the ICU."

"Well, I'll be dipped," I reply. "I guess I lucked out."

"Guess so," she says as she shuffles past Jeff and messes around with my IV bag. "How's your pain?"

"Better now that you're here," I say in an attempt to flirt. At first, I think it falls flat, but she smiles and lets out a snort.

"I'm glad I could help," she says as she changes out the bag. "Mind if I get your vitals?"

"Sure," I reply, and she walks out to the hall for a moment and comes in with a little machine, pulling it behind her.

"What's all that for? I'm already hooked to this EKG machine."

"I use the pulse tool for your oxygen levels, not just your pulse," she says as she starts pulling things out. "I'll need to check your temperature as well. Open wide!"

I obey, opening my mouth, but when she leans in close, I'm hit with a whiff of her lovely perfume. Moving to check my pulse, she puts the monitor on my finger, and the machine starts to beep—my heart is racing from her being so close.

"Are you feeling okay?" she asks as she sees the number, and immediately I feel embarrassed as I had set off both the vitals card and the heart monitor.

"Yeah, yeah," I reply. "Just excited to maybe get these bandages off today."

"Ooh! Then we'll be able to see your handsome face," she says with a smile as the blood pressure cuff pumps up. She waits, watching the screen until it deflates, and the numbers show. She then pulls a notepad out of her pocket and appears to write it all down.

"You know, I keep trying to remember where I know you from," I say as I stare at her, trying desperately to put the pieces together. But once again, nothing is coming. "Where did we meet?"

She stops writing and looks up at me; I can see tears start to form in her eyes.

Shoot, I didn't mean to make her upset.

"Well, that's it for me," she says, seeming to dodge my question. It's so odd. It's okay that I see Darla, and that I talk to her, but everyone's keeping quiet about who she is. *She's obviously someone important to me if Zack and Noah brought her in to see me,* I think to myself as she slips the notepad into her scrubs pocket. *I just wish I knew why...*

"I'll be back around later, okay?" she says.

"I'll look forward to it," I reply, and the smile returns to her face as she grabs the vitals cart and pulls it out the door.

"The way you flirt with her, you'd think you'd remember her," Noah teases as he walks in.

"I wish," I reply with a sigh. "She does seem familiar though, I just can't quite put my finger on it."

"Like the doctor said, it'll all come back in time he thinks," Jeffrey says. "Try not to sweat it, I'm sure you'll figure it out."

"Yeah, relax a bit," Zack insists as he walks in and stands next to Noah. "You'll get it, I'm sure of it."

"Get what?" I ask, and the room goes quiet. "What is it that I'm not remembering?"

"I think we should tell him," Noah says.

"No!" Jeffrey growls. "The doctor says he needs his rest, and to let it all come naturally!"

"Now that's enough," I say, getting frustrated and slightly raising my voice, causing the boys to all snap to attention. "I know what that doctor says, but it's ridiculous that you three are constantly talking in code about this woman. I want to know what the deal is!"

Everyone goes silent again. Dead silent. The only sounds are the quiet beeps from the heart monitor.

"Dad, Darla isn't just anyone," Zack replies, "she's your girlfriend."

"What?" I ask, my jaw dropping in surprise. "I'm dating someone?"

"Yes," Noah replies. "It's sort of new but I mean, Mom's been gone ten years. You said you felt it was time."

Wow, I think to myself. *I can't believe that I'd start dating again after Mel. I'd been heartbroken for so long, hung up on her. What changed?*

"How did I meet her?" I ask, and the two boys start to chuckle a bit.

"The first time, or when you started dating?" Zack asks with a grin and Noah nudges him in the ribs.

"Let him try to remember that part on his own," Noah replies.

"Mitch told you about this dating app, and y'all started talking," Zack says. "Then you guys went out on some dates, and the day of the accident you made it official."

"The ranch hand told me about it?" I ask.

"Mm-hmm," Noah agrees.

"Wow... me, on a dating app?" I say with a laugh. "That's so weird."

"A bit," Noah says with a nod. "But whatever makes you happy is fine with us."

I'm absolutely blown away. *I have a girlfriend, of all things,* I think to myself, and then I suddenly feel a gnawing at the pit of my stomach.

Guilt.

It's no wonder why that poor woman is on the verge of tears half the time she's around me, I think to myself. *I mean, honestly, that has to be so hard, being with someone who doesn't remember you. It's even worse because she seems so nice, on top of being a total babe.*

My brain really needs to kick into gear. Losing a woman like her would be tragic.

I ran into the bathroom after leaving Eli's room, closed myself into the stall, and started to cry. It's hard hearing him flirt with me when I feel so deeply for him, and he doesn't even recall what we have. As if what we had wasn't ever real, only my imagination.

However, I don't have time to sit around and mope, I have work to do. Both with my other patients and snooping on the hospital computer.

Oddly enough, my friend in the IT department at the hospital back home had taught me how to hack into the systems to look at things if I needed to. Mostly because I'd had a sneaking suspicion before I found the beast and the harlot together that something may have been amiss. However, it helped with other things too—like seeing schedules or peeking at patient records. It wasn't something I would normally do, but I needed to know what was going on with the Eli debacle. Because the more I thought about it, the more it just didn't make sense.

I'm not sure if my little skillset will work at Thistleberry Medical, but they use the same system as back home. So, it's safe to assume that it will. And when I finally get a free moment and the other girls are busy, I pounce at the chance to dig up some information.

I steal a cautionary glance around the ward before I sink my teeth into it, tinkering around with the computer. At first, I'm unsure if I can get the access I need, but then I enter the repair tech's login that I remembered.

Bingo.

We are in baby.

Okay, Elijah Garcia... edited two days ago, deceased. Editing was done by... Doctor Trachner. That tracks. But there's no trail leading back to the prior edit.

Strange, there should be.

I switch to Eli's record, and I root around like a pig looking for truffles in the dirt. Once again, I can see the edit from Doctor Trachner, this time approved by the head of the hospital, Doctor Joseph Harrison... and then my eyes pop open when I see it.

Doctor Joseph Harrison was the one to override the edit and switch Eli and Elijah.

But why? Why would the head of the hospital do such a thing, and intentionally? I need to speak to Doctor Harrison and see what the deal is.

"Hey, Rosita?" I call out as she passes by.

"Yes?"

"I need like half an hour, I have to talk to HR about an issue," I say. "Are you and Heather okay?"

"Yeah, that's fine," she replies. "Just try to be back before rounds. Ms. Keenan is really testy and demanding."

"Sure, of course," I say as I log out of the computer and hurry to the elevator. Something about this stinks like a scared polecat, and I want to know why.

As the metal box lurches to a halt at the top floor, every muscle in my body feels so tense it's like I'm on fire. The door slowly slides open, and I exit. Even though I know this is the only way to figure this thing out, I'm scared to death of taking it head on.

As much as I love Eli, I really need this job. It's what's keeping my house afloat and food on my table. So, as I walk to the receptionist's desk, I'm already trying to come up with a scheme as to how I can be both sweet and direct at the same time. One false move that the director doesn't like, and that could mean the unemployment line.

"Can I help you?" the young lady at the desk asks.

"Yes, I'm Darla from the ICU," I say. "I'm here to see Doctor Harrison about an important matter."

"Do you have an appointment?" she asks as she sifts through the paperwork on her desk.

"It's an emergency situation so, no, I can't say that I do," I reply.

"Well then you'll have to try to make an appointment," she says. "I'm sure we have some openings next week—"

"I don't think I made myself clear enough," I say, taking some of the syrupy sweetness out of my voice. "It's urgent."

"So are all of the other staff's problems Ms...."

"Darla Middleton," I reply dryly, getting irritated with her attitude. "And I don't think that their problems are the intentional switching of two patients under the director's name, are they?"

The lady at the desk gets really quiet. I can tell she's shocked but trying hard not to show it. "Have a seat, Ms. Middleton, I'll let him know you're here."

CHAPTER SEVENTEEN

I do just that, flopping down in the armchair closest to me, if you could call it that. It feels like I'm sitting on the floor, and the minutes that tick by seem to drag on until a man comes out in a suit and smiles at me.

Immediately, I recognize him, and it takes me back a bit when I realize that I recognize him from Moonshine and Music. He'd been hanging with Joseph, my ex, the night that Eli had told him off.

"You're Ms. Darla, I take it?" he asks, his hands shaking a bit as he adjusts his tie.

"Yes sir," I reply as I stand up. Much to my surprise, he doesn't waste time, strolling over to shake my hand. His palm is surprisingly clammy with perspiration.

It's obvious he's just as nervous as I am, which makes me feel a lot better about coming to him. It's possible he's just as in the dark as I am about the whole thing. I'm just hoping that I won't be seen as a troublemaker.

"Shall we step into my office?" he says as he waves me toward the door he came out of, and I file in after him.

"Have a seat," he says, motioning to the chairs in front of his gigantic, cherry wood desk.

"Thank you," I reply.

"Now, Tessa tells me that you're here about the Garcia debacle," Doctor Harrison says as he takes a seat in his high-backed, cushioned seat.

"Yes actually, I am," I say as I sit up straight in my seat, hoping that I am exuding the confidence my voice feigns. "Something is truly bothering me about this situation."

"Same here," Doctor Harrison says with a sigh. "I've been investigating the situation all day, and I've done all I can to figure out who accessed my credentials. I even brought in the technician, and we are all stumped."

"When I looked, you were the only login," I say, and I half expect him to ask how I know that.

"Well, I can assure you I certainly wouldn't do anything like that," Doctor Harrison insists, surprising me when he doesn't question what I know. "This is my career we are talking about. If Elijah's family decides to sue, I'm in a heap of trouble. I really feel terrible for them, no one should be put through that."

I can sense from the panic and sorrow in his voice that he's being sincere. It wouldn't make sense for him to do something so foolish. But he is friends with Joseph...

"How long have you known Joseph Middleton?" I ask.

"Joe? You related?" he asks.

"You could say that," I say as I force a smile.

"Since college, actually," he says. "We used to be very close, but once I moved down here, we lost touch."

I don't remember him from college, but I suppose that doesn't mean much. I mean, I thought I knew the man I married, and I clearly didn't. So, it's not too farfetched that I'd never met him.

"I see," I say. "He's my ex-husband.""He had a wife?" Doctor Harrison says, seeming to be genuinely shocked. "News to me. I remember a girlfriend, but I never met her."

"That would be me," I say, trying to be careful of what I reveal. I can't entirely trust this man, not yet. "But we are divorced now."

"So weird," he says, and we sit there for a moment in awkward, uncomfortable silence. Until finally, another idea wafts through my head. A horrible realization. *Joseph had said that he would make me regret not taking him back. . . Would he be capable of doing something to the records?*

"Doctor Harrison, can you access the hospitals records and system from home?" I ask.

"Yes, actually," he replies. "But it's supposed to be safe."

Not if you know how to crack it. And if I do, then maybe Joseph does too.

"Where do you keep the computer?" I ask.

"In my office," he replies. "Locked up at all times."

"And no one in your home or anyone that may have visited would have had access to it?" I ask, and his face sours.

"Listen, Ms. Middleton, I appreciate you trying to help, but what we really need at this time is to keep this quiet until it's sorted," Doctor Harrison insists, not even bothering to answer my question. "But if you hear anything more, please let me know."

"Of course," I say. "You have my utmost cooperation. I wouldn't want something like this to happen again."

"I appreciate it," he says as I get up to leave. *It's obvious from his reaction that he knows it might not have been kept as secure as he claims*, I think to myself. So, now it really is on me to get to the bottom of it. Like Nancy Drew, I'm going to crack the case no matter what. Both Eli and Elijah deserve justice.

Chapter Eighteen

Skylar White
Clean Romance

ELI

"Eli! How's my best buddy doing today?" Mitch says as he walks into my room, interrupting the mindless boredom I've been stuck in since the boys left.

"Hey there," I say, flashing him a smile.

"Well look at you, no more peeking at you through all those wraps," Mitch replies, pointing to my head.

"Yeah, but they shaved my head and I look like a doofus," I say with a sigh. "But it feels better this way than with those bandages on."

"Eh, it's only hair," he replies with a shrug, "it'll grow back."

"I suppose you're right. But until then, I'm definitely not winning any beauty contests, that's for sure," I say with a chuckle.

"I don't know, there's plenty of pretty bald men and women out there," Mitch teases.

"Yeah, but I'm not interested in other women," I say.

"Oh?"

"I've actually got my eye on someone here," I say.

"Really?" Mitch replies. "Who's the lucky gal?"

"Mm-hmm, one of the nurses here, actually," I say.

"Well dang, Cassanova! Good for you!" Mitch says with a mile-wide grin, sitting down next to me.

"You might know her," I say. "I guess I'm supposed to, too. . ."

"Please tell me you ain't talking about that Darla, are you?"

"Actually, I am," I reply. "She's an amazing nurse."

"She's a maternity ward nurse, what is she doing down here?" Mitch asks, seemingly shocked. "She hates ICU work."

"Not sure, but this is where she works," I say with a shrug. "According to the boys, she's my girlfriend. . . Or she was, before the accident."

"Eli—"

"You know, I'm not too sure how to proceed with all of this as I am now but I gotta say, I ain't too mad about it."

"Eli, Darla is not who you think she is," Mitch says with a sigh, his face going from happy-go-lucky and grinning to concerned, fast enough to make your head spin.

"Why? What's wrong with her?" I ask.

"She's a maneater, that's what's wrong with her," Mitch says. "She likes to mess with your head, chew you up, and spit you out like you're nothin'. I've told you this before!"

I can sense the anger and vitriol spewing out in his bashing of Darla, and it leaves me feeling confused. . . but he's made it clear we've discussed this before.

"Maybe you've forgotten but I have amnesia, Mitch," I reply. "I hardly remember you, to be fair."

"Sorry, I just don't want you to get hurt," Mitch says. "She's an awful person."

"How would you even know that? Did you date her?" I ask, and he immediately looks repulsed and anxious.

"What, me?" Mitch asks, pointing to himself and laughing nervously. "No way, no! My buddy, Joe—"

"From the bar," I say as a flash of a memory peeks through. "Joseph, from the bar. I went to tell him off, and you said you'd talk to him about following her around, right?"

"Well, yeah, but—"

"You're good friends with him, so you're already biased," I say. "If I'm remembering correctly, we've also already spoken about his bad deeds before. He's not without sin either, and honestly, he seems to be the villain here. So, with all things considered, I don't understand why you hate her so much."

"Eli, it's a bit more complicated than all that," Mitch stammers. "And we aren't supposed to get you all riled up."

"Well, it's a bit too late for that," I say, feeling a bit angry at his poor attitude toward Darla. "I may not remember everything, but I know how I feel about her, and you should respect that."

The room falls silent, the only sound coming from the television, the murmurs of the cowboys in the western I'd been watching on and off droning on in the background. Mitch looks off toward the window, as if he's deep in thought, before shaking his head. "Well, I better get going," he says suddenly.

"What? But you just got here," I say, raising my brow. *I really must have upset him more than I thought.*

"I've got some stuff to take care of," Mitch replies as he gets up. "Take 'er easy, Eli," he says before he disappears out into the hallway. . . and there's something about his weird, erratic behavior that leaves me with an odd sense of unease.

Rosita is going to be so irritated with me, I think to myself as I look down at the time on my phone. That took way longer than a half hour. I sigh as the doors slide open. My eyes immediately scan the hall, looking to see if I can find Rosita to apologize. *Guess she's in a patient's room*, I think as I walk back onto the ward and get to the nurse's desk, just in time to see a familiar face.

Joseph's face, and he's coming out of Eli's room.

Panic immediately sets in, and I duck down as he walks by, his cowboy boots clicking loudly on the tile. *What is he doing here? And why was he in Eli's room?*

I need to find out.

Poor Rosita will have to wait. After I glance toward Eli's room and see that none of the machines are going off, and that he's preoccupied with the TV, I stalk down the hall after Joe. After seeing him, I have a horrible feeling that it really is all connected to Joseph.

Quietly tip toeing down the hall—glad I was wearing flats—I watch from a pillar as he boards the elevator, waiting for the door to close before flying as fast as I can down the stairs, hoping I won't lose him in the shuffle of the hospital. Thankfully, however, once I reach the bottom floor and peer out the doorway, I can still see him a few steps ahead of me. So, like a lion on the prowl, I creep after him into the parking lot.

For once, I'm glad that I have to park farther out to make the walk to the hospital shorter for the patients when I realize that whatever he's driving, our cars are in the same area. I duck and weave between cars, making sure not to be seen as he gets in his car, and I make a mad dash for my own.

I need to know where he's going, I think to myself. There's no reason for him to be anywhere near Eli.

Ever.

I get to the back of my car, and I squat down, watching him as he sits there. Luckily, he takes a moment before he leaves, and as he slowly pulls out of his spot, I scramble for my front seat. I twist the key in my ignition, praying that it'll start, and when it does, I am in hot pursuit.

I quickly put on some sunglasses as I follow closely behind, but I'm still sweating bullets when we have to stop at a light. I duck down and try to find the ascot that I had worn out one day. When I find it, I wrap it around my hair as well, trying to hide my identity the best that I can.

Lucky for me, Joe doesn't look back at all, seeming to be far too focused on getting to wherever it is that he needs to go. So much so that I almost lose him three different times once he speeds into the hills, hitting about eighty.

Where is he going in such a hurry? I ask myself as I continue to tail him. *Does he live out this way?* But then he takes a sudden turn up a very familiar dirt road, and my mind feels like it might explode.

He's going to Eli's.

I wait until he's just out of sight before turning onto the dirt road, and then I scoot up it myself, my heart pounding. *What could he possibly be doing here?* I ask myself. *The boys are probably there. . . Is he going to hurt them? They may not be my kids, but I care about them immensely. I'm not about to let some psycho ex of mine touch one hair on their heads.*

I watch him park in front of the house, and I speed up, my tires screeching as I come to a halt right behind him as he angrily stomps toward the house. I get out my phone and fumble with it a minute, taking a picture as he turns to look at me, his eyes wide as I get out of the car and slam the door.

"Joseph Rutherford Middleton!" I scream as I march right up to him, blocking his path to the door. "What do you think you're doing here?"

"Darla, you need to move," he replies as he tries to push past me, but I bob and weave and continue to obstruct him from going any further.

"No! You're going to tell me what is going on here!" I yell. Behind me I hear the porch door open, and I glance over my shoulder to see the boys, Zack and Noah, standing on the porch.

"Darla?" Zack asks.

"Zack, don't move," I say. "This man isn't right in the head, and I don't want you to get hurt."

"Darla!" Joseph hollers at me, pushing his chest into mine. "I said, move!"

"I'm not going anywhere until you tell me what in the blue blazes is going on here," I growl, standing firm. "Why are you at Eli's, Joseph?"

"Who's Joseph?" Noah asks.

"Yeah, that's Mitch," Zack says, looking extremely confused.

"Mitch? No, his name is Joseph," I reply, my eyes flickering right back to Joseph who looks absolutely mortified. "And he's my ex-husband."

"Seriously?" Zack asks, shifting uncomfortably where he stands, and Zack crosses his arms tightly across his chest.

"She's crazy," Joseph stutters. "I told you all she was crazy!"

"I'm not crazy, you are!" I insist. "You mean to tell me you've been working here as Eli's ranch hand?" As I look him over closely, I remember the man in the barn, the one that Eli had called Mitch. "Jeezum crow! You were the guy in the bandana on Valentine's Day, watching us while you worked!"

"I—"

"Is this true?" Zack asks. "Are you who she says you are?"

"No! Of course not," Joseph insists as he rifles through his pants pocket, pulls out his ID, and holds it up. "You see? I'm Mitch!"

"And who did you pay to have that done?" I ask as I snatch it out of his hand. "It's pretty well made, but the corners are already starting to come apart."

"Darla, you need to let me through so I can get to my room. I've had enough of your insanity for a lifetime," Joseph says as he tries once again to move past me, but I refuse to budge.

"No," I say as I stand firmly in his way. "You're going to explain to me what's going on. Why are you working here? What's your angle?"

"I've got no angle," Joseph says as he glares at me. "Joe warned me you were psychotic, but this takes the cake."

"Stop your lying and fess up!" I demand.

"Can't fess up to a delusional lie now, can I?" Joe says with a shrug as he takes a step forward. "Now move."

"If I'm so delusional, Joe, what's this?" I ask as I pull my phone back out, go to my social media, and pull up our wedding photo. I hold it up in his face, and his eyes grow wide as I turn around and show the boys. Pointing to the caption. "See? That's me and that's him, Nurse Darla Middleton and Doctor Joseph Middleton."

"Oh my God. . ." Noah says. "I knew there was something fishy about you!"

"Boys, it's not what it looks like," Joseph insists as the boys slowly make their way toward us.

"What it looks like is that you're working here to stalk Darla," Zack says.

"That's not true!" Joseph says. "Remember? I'm the one that told him about the dating app!"

"Maybe it didn't start that way," I interject. "Maybe you didn't mean for him to find me on there, because you were so sure I'd take you back you didn't think I'd be on there. But even then, why find work around Thistleberry? Why follow me all the way here and keep harassing me if you weren't sticking around here to stalk me?" I ask.

"Just keep your mouth shut!" Joseph yells.

"You came to my house, you begged me to take you back, you followed me to the bar when we went on our date. . ." I say. "If you realized that he was dating me. . . No, with how close you got to Eli, you'd easily know that, wouldn't you?"

"I swear if you don't shut your mouth, Darla. . ." Joseph growls, and then I feel a hand on my shoulder as Zack steps in front of me, shielding me from Joseph's growing anger. His face turns as red as a ripened tomato, and the vein near his temple pulses.

"Or what, Mitch?" Zack asks Joseph. "Or should I say Joe? What exactly do you think you're going to do?"

"Back off, Zack," Joseph insists. "You're not part of this."

"Oh no, I think we are," Noah says. "It all makes sense now. Constantly talking poorly about Darla, getting angry with Dad every time he'd go out with her. . ."

Noah gets quiet for a moment, and then his eyes widen. "It was you," he says as he walks in front of Zack, pointing at Joe. "It was you that caused the stampede, you caused Tango to rear up!"

"Have you completely lost your mind, Noah?" Joseph asks, but he is sweating bullets. "Why would I do that?"

"To get to me. . ." I say as I have my own terrible realization that my suspicions were true. "And you're the one who changed the records at the hospital!"

"No!"

"You're friends with Joseph Harrison, the head of the hospital, he confirmed it himself," I say, peering at him from behind the boys. "We had the same hospital system back home. You stole his credentials somehow and changed the info to hurt me and make me think he was dead. . ."

"I'm telling you she's wrong!"

"You thought I was working maternity, didn't you?" I ask as all the puzzle pieces fall together in my mind. "You didn't realize I'd be working the ICU. . ."

"You tried to kill him twice you coward!" Zack yells angrily, launching himself at Joseph and landing a punch to his cheek before the two of them topple to the ground.

"Get off of me!" Joseph howls as they roll around, dirt flying everywhere as Zack's arm hunkers back and he throws another punch, only for Joseph to block it and toss a handful of dirt in his eyes.

"Zack!" Noah yells as Joseph scrambles to his feet. Noah pursues him, launching his body forward and grabbing Joseph around his legs. As the two of them tussle on the ground, I get out my phone and call the police.

"Hello? Nine-one-one, what's your emergency?" the operator asks as I watch Noah and Joseph fight, Noah overpowering Joseph.

"I need a car sent to 641 Texas Rose Lane," I reply, hands shaking. "My ex-husband tried to kill my current boyfriend! He's been living in their house and now he's in a fight with his kids!"

"Ma'am, I don't understand," the operator says. "Slow down and—"

"We don't have time to slow down!" I say. "This man here tried to kill someone! And who knows what he's going to do next! You have to get hurry while he's still here!"

"Ma'am—" the operator says, and I watch as Joseph kicks Noah off of him finally, and Noah falls over on his side and grunts in pain.

"You're going to regret this, Darla," Joseph says with a snicker. "If I'm going down, I'm going down swinging."

Joseph rushes to his car, gets in, and quickly pulls off.

"Dang it!" I say as I run toward my car.

"Ma'am? What's going on?"

"Tell the cops to head to Thistleberry Medical," I say.

"Previously, you requested—"

"I know what I said dang it," I say, out of breath as I rush to my car. "He said I'm going to regret this, and I have a patient at the hospital, my boyfriend, that he already tried to kill once in the ICU."

"Ma'am, I need you to remain calm—"

"Just please!" I say as I turn my car on and pull out, speeding after Joseph. I see him in the distance, and I throw all my worries about my own self-preservation to the side as I slam the pedal down to the floor.

"For clarification, you are now requesting that we send officers to Thistleberry Medical, ICU unit?" they ask as Joseph makes a sharp turn and I follow suit. But I'm soon lost in his dust, and I slam my hand on the steering wheel.

"Shoot!" I say as I continue to drive.

"Someone's been shot?" the dispatcher asks.

"No! But I don't know what he's capable of," I groan. "Just send your people to the hospital!"

Chapter Nineteen

ELI

Attempting to shake off Mitch's odd departure, I lay in bed, watching a little television while I tried to eat the lunch one of the nurses brought in. *Man, I'll be glad when I'm home,* I think to myself as I bite down on a bit of turkey. As I chew it, I nearly choke. Even with gravy, it's far too dry and hard to eat.

I miss home. I miss sleeping in my bed. I miss my boys. I even miss cooking us all breakfast every morning before we go out to feed the animals, lunch at midday, and dinner when it's all done. It's weird. I never thought I'd miss cooking of all things, but here we are.

As I take a sip of my orange juice, Doctor Trachner comes in, all smiles with his clipboard in his hand.

"Hey there, Doc," I say as I abandon the English muffin and try to tackle the eggs.

"Good morning, Eli!" he says as he takes one of the chairs and sits down. "How are you feeling?"

"Pretty good," I say as I take a bite of the mashed potatoes and stuffing, and try my best not to make a face, not wanting to be rude. "Got some headaches going on, but I suppose that's to be expected, considering."

"And I read you've been up and walking?" Doctor Trachner asks.

"Yep! I go walking any chance I can get with some help from the nurses," I say. "I've got to get used to moving around again, I've got lots of animals at home to help care for."

"That's kind of what I came in to talk to you about," Doctor Trachner says. "I believe you've been making great strides, and by next week, as long as we keep on this path, you may be able to return home."

"Really?" I reply, sitting up in bed, nearly toppling over my orange juice as I knock into the tray.

"Yes sir," Doctor Trachner says with a big ol' smile on his face. "I mean, it won't be without restrictions, but nothing too limiting."

"Restrictions?" I ask.

"You won't be able to do any heavy work for a few months, and you'll have to do some outpatient physical therapy and do regular check-ins with a neurologist due to your memory loss. We want to do our best to prevent the worsening of brain function and be proactive about any potential future issues from the damage to your brain. But you'll be able to go home."

"I suppose I can handle that," I say with a grin. "Not that you all haven't been amazing, but I really need to get back."

"Understandable," Doctor Trachner replies. "Well then, I'll be keeping a close eye on you, and hopefully everything will go according to plan."

"That would be amazing," I say.

"I'll leave you to your lunch," Doctor Trachner says as he gets up from his chair and leans over, holding his hand out to me. I shake it, and when he turns and leaves, I nearly whoop loudly in celebration.

I can't believe I'm going home soon! I think to myself. It's been too long with me sitting around here like a bump on a log. I want to go home, be with my family, and see where life takes me.

And I want to see Darla again, not just inside these hospital walls either, but properly. I remember our night at Moonshine and Music now, thanks to Mitch's tantrum about her. But I don't just recall the night, but the feelings I felt and still feel about her. I might not ever remember everything, but I'm hopeful in time that I will. But, even if I don't, I still feel those butterflies when I see her, and I want to explore that.

It's been so long since I've felt like this about another person, and after everything that's happened, I want to keep that feeling for myself. Life can be cut short in an instant, and with this second chance I've been given, I want to live mine to the fullest.

CHAPTER NINETEEN

"Hey there." I hear someone call to me from the door, interrupting my train of thought. When I look up, Mitch is standing there, oddly sweaty from his forehead to his pits.

"Hey, thought you had stuff to do?" I ask and Mitch takes a few more steps in.

"Oh, I did," Mitch says, his cowboy boots clicking with each step, and I notice he seems upset. Glaring at me like he's angry with me. *I guess I did go at him a little hard earlier about Darla...*

"You okay?" I ask. "You're acting strange."

Without skipping a beat, Mitch looks up to the privacy curtain rail and pulls the curtain around us. "I was at the ranch and Darla showed up."

"Oh! She was probably just checking up on the boys," I reply. "She's been worried about them."

"She followed me home, Eli," Mitch says, shaking his head. "She's accusing me of being Joseph."

"Her ex?" I ask, instantly confused. "Why would she do that?"

"I know!" Mitch replies, stepping closer. "I told you she's lost her mind. She's a complete psycho!"

"That doesn't seem right..." I whisper to myself as he moves closer.

"I don't understand why you won't just listen to me, Eli," Mitch says. "If you had, things wouldn't be the way they are."

"I beg your pardon?" I say as he's closing in, and I see the evil in his eyes when I hear the door behind him slam open. Darla rips the curtain to the side so hard she pulls half of it off of the track.

"Get away from him, Joseph!" Darla yells loudly.

"Darla! Shut your mouth!" Mitch screams back at her, his voice cracking with desperation. "You see? Insane!"

"I'm not crazy!" Darla insists. "Step away from Eli, Joseph. You're not thinking straight. You need to calm down and back away."

"Shut up, woman!" Mitch roars as he turns to her for a second, taking his cowboy hat off and tossing it angrily to the ground. "You need to mind your business!"

"Mitch is Joseph, my ex-husband," Darla says quietly, her voice shaking despite her best attempts to stay cool and even. "And somehow, he changed the records to make you seem like you'd died. I know it's a lot to take in right now, but I swear on my life, it's true."

"What?" I ask, dumbfounded.

"See? She's cracked!" Mitch insists, but then Darla pushes past him and pushes her phone into my face.

"Look," she says, and I study the photo. It's a wedding photo that I've never seen before, at least not that I can remember, but two things are true. That's Darla in that wedding dress, and next to her in a tuxedo with a big grin on his face is Mitch.

No.

Underneath it says. . . Joseph. Doctor Joseph Middleton.

"What the—"

"You just couldn't die, could you?" Joseph growls, and I feel pain streak through my head as I remember Joseph on the day of the stampede. . . the words he'd said to me as he pushed me off my horse.

It's really too bad you couldn't take the hint, cowboy. . . now I've got to take you out of the equation."

Oh my gosh. . . this man is Joseph. . . and he really did try to kill me! I think to myself. I hear a click, and when I look up, I realize I'm looking down the cold barrel of a gun that Joseph has thrusted into my face.

"Put the gun down, Joseph," I say calmly as I go to stand up.

"Don't move another muscle," Joseph says, his face crimson with anger, and his finger wobbling over the trigger.

"I don't think you really want to do this," I insist, still slowly moving to a standing position as I feel the EKG nodules pop one by one off my chest, and the machine begins to beep wildly.

"I don't know about that," Joseph says. "Seems pretty cut and dry to me, Eli. You're in my way. You wouldn't stop seeing my wife, now here we are."

"Joe, put the gun down," I repeat again quietly, treating him like a wounded, wound up, unpredictable horse that could kick at any second. It's obvious he's lost it, and I need to try to diffuse the situation as best I can to make sure that no one gets hurt. But what I am most worried about is that he's so far gone he'll go after Darla.

"And what are you going to do if I don't, captain brain damage?" Joseph asks with a chuckle.

Suddenly, Darla pulls on his arm, and when he turns to look, I take my opportunity to pounce, side stepping to avoid a bullet if the gun went off. I lock up his wrist, and slam my elbow down into his, causing Joe to lose his grip.

CHAPTER NINETEEN 139

The gun clatters to the ground, and we both dive for it, struggling against one another on the floor. Gaining control, I kick him in the ribs, and I'm able to grab the gun as I shakily sit up, my blood pumping as I level the gun and train it between his eyes.

***

"Don't move," Eli says as he stands up slowly and motions for me to come closer. I slip past Joseph, scared out of my mind as Joseph pushes me behind him. Protecting me from Joe.

"We both know you aren't going to shoot me," Joseph says with a chuckle. "You don't have the guts, Eli."

"Apparently you don't know me as well as you think you do," Eli says. "But I guess that's something we have in common, isn't it?"

"You're too much of a softie, Eli," Joseph replies, his voice dripping with venom. "Pathetic, really. Pining over your dead wife while stealing someone else's."

"You've truly lost it," Eli replies, shaking his head. "You're the one who cheated and took off, and the last time I checked, Darla divorced you. Unlike you, I'd never be such a low life. I take care of my family, and I'd do anything for them. . . and the woman I love."

My heart skips a beat, and I peer at Joseph who looks like he's truly lost his mind. His eyes are wild, and he looks utterly disheveled.

"You think you're better than me?" Joseph yells, and I'm waiting for him to lunge at us at any moment, but it never comes, the cops bursting through the door with guns drawn.

"TPD! Put the gun down!" one of the officers yell.

"Yeah, Eli, put the gun down," Joseph replies smugly. Eli clicks the safety back on, holds it to his side, and drops it to the floor.

"He was only defending himself," I say. "He's the one you want. That's Joseph Rutherford Middleton! He's wanted by the police for several crimes, and he's tried to murder this man in cold blood."

"She doesn't know what she's talking about," Joseph insists. "She's lost it!" I then hold up my phone, and I hit play.

"You're going to regret this, Darla," my phone chimes, and Joseph whips around and glares at me.

"You little—"

"I'm Darla," I say. "I'm the one who called. Mr. Middleton came here to try and kill him. The gun is his."

The room is tense for a few moments, and I hold my breath as the officer trains his gun on us, looking around the room.

"I need confirmation on warrants for a Joseph Middleton," he says as he leans his head toward his shoulder, speaking into his walkie talkie.

"You've got to be kidding," Joseph mutters.

"Confirmed," someone says over the radio, and the cop switches gears and points his gun at Joseph.

"Joseph Middleton, you are under arrest for suspected attempted murder, medical tampering, and several other crimes," the cop says as he steps forward, and a part of me expects Joseph to fight. Instead, he hangs his head in defeat as the cop reads him his Miranda rights, clamps the handcuffs on Joseph's wrists, and leads him out of the room.

"Thank God," I say as Eli turns around, and I can't help but hop into his arms. He holds me tight. "I thought I was going to lose you."

"Well, I survived this, being dead, and a stampede... I'd say the odds are in my favor," Eli jokes with a chuckle as he kisses my forehead. "I'm just glad you're alright."

"Do you remember me now?" I ask as I let go a little and look up at him.

"I remember enough," he says with a smile as he stares lovingly into my eyes, his gorgeous smile back on his face. The one that crinkles the corners of his brilliant blue eyes.

"Did you mean what you said?" I ask.

"About what?"

"Loving me," I say, and he beams a bit brighter.

"Darla, you make my heart sing in a way I haven't felt in a very long time," Eli says as he puts his hand to my cheek, and gently rubs it with his thumb. "I do love you, and I want to see where the future takes us."

"Even after all this?" I ask, as tears fall down my cheeks.

"Even after all this," he replies as he leans down, pressing his lips to mine as nurses and a doctor pile into the room, along with a cop, all to check on Eli. But he doesn't let go. He just keeps kissing me like no one is watching, and I hold onto him tighter.

I never want to let go again.

Epilogue

Skylar White
Clean Romance

DARLA

The early morning sun beats into my eyes as I sit up with a yawn, Eli still asleep next to me. *Shoot, my alarm clock never went off!* I think to myself as I rush to get dressed, pulling the clothes I'd brought with me out of my little travel bag and hurrying off to the bathroom to shower.

Although I have my own house, I stay with Eli and the boys most nights. While things between the two of us are grand to say the least, we are still taking it all somewhat slow, just living life and enjoying every moment the best we can. And having my own house still feels like the safety net I need, even though more than a year has passed.

All the boys are home for Christmas, including Robert, and my son, Little Joe, is here too, spending the night in one of the rooms at Eli's ranch. Sparrow, Daniel, and baby Jade are coming too. Except she's not so much a baby anymore, toddling around and terrorizing her mama—which I constantly tease Sparrow about. Telling her it's retribution for all she'd put me through in her terrible twos.

I speed through my shower, get dressed, head out to the kitchen, and pop an apron on so I don't ruin my dress. I preheat the oven, pull the ham out of the fridge and put it on the counter, open up a new package of brown sugar, and begin rubbing it all over the outside. Everyone loves candied ham, and though I am nervous about getting everything right, not much can go sideways with that.

Or at least, I hope.

Soon as it's preheated, I throw it in the oven and begin peeling potatoes to mash when I hear footsteps come up behind me, and feel arms slide around my waist.

"I told you to wake me up, darlin'," Eli says as he squeezes me tight, kissing me on the cheek before he takes the peeler out of my hand.

"I know, but you were actually sleeping in for once," I say with a sigh.

"Animals still got to be fed, Darla," Eli replies. "And you need help with dinner."

"Actually, animals are all accounted for," Zack says as he comes through the front door, Noah following in right behind.

"We got up early to grab 'em so you could relax," Noah says with a grin.

"That's so sweet of the two of you," I say with a smile.

"Yes, thank you boys," Eli says as he begins to peel the potatoes.

"Anything we can help with?" Zack asks.

"No, I think I've got it covered," I say. "You boys might want to shower and get dressed so you don't smell like a barn though."

"Ten-four, step mama," Zack says with a wink, and the two boys wander off, leaving Eli and I to prepare for an early Christmas dinner. More like lunch, I suppose. We wanted to make sure that all the other Christmas festivities weren't overshadowed by the food.

Eventually, everyone else wakes up, and I keep shuffling things around as Eli gets breakfast ready for everybody. After that, I get the sides ready to go into the oven about a half hour before we're going to eat—yams, green bean casserole, baked beans, and all that—plus, there's stuffing, collards, and mashed potatoes I still have to make on the stovetop.

Sparrow finally shows up with Daniel and Jade at about one o' clock, and by that time I have everything done and spread out on the large kitchen table. Luckily there's plenty of seats, and all of us dine together happily, talking amongst one another and having a good ol' time.

After everyone is nearly in a food coma, we sit with Jade and watch all the old Christmas classics—Rudolph, Frosty, and more—until the pies are ready, and everyone goes back into the kitchen to peruse the desserts. Cookies, cakes, candies, and pies. I've made enough to feed our small platoon of kids, and enough to send them home with, that's for sure.

Then, it's finally time for what everyone has been patiently waiting for—present time. It's my favorite time, honestly, besides the food. Getting to see the joy on everyone's faces as they peel back that wrapping paper to find something they'll love.

I was sure I had nailed Noah, Zack, and even Jeffrey's presents since I knew them so well now. But Robert was a bit of a wild card, and as we got to him, I held my breath since I'd taken a stab in the dark.

"Oh wow, workout clothes, I've been needing these!" Robert says with a smile. "I love them Darla, thank you."

"You're welcome," I say as I return the smile. "Well, that's all for gifts!" I say as I watch Jade play with her toys in a pile of wrapping paper.

"Not true," Eli says. "We haven't traded gifts."

"We have so," I reply. "I got you a bunch of stuff right there."

"Yes, well, I'm not done," Eli says with a shrug.

"What? You already got me these beautiful earrings and the dress I'm wearing," I reply. "That's more than enough."

"Well, I can't exactly take this one back," Eli says with a chuckle. "But it requires everyone to get their coats on, and it's not just from me really, it's from everyone."

I'm confused, but I get up and put on my coat, and everyone else follows suit, with impish smiles on their faces. Eli pulls a bandana out of his pocket, and then twirls me around.

"Gotta make sure you don't peek," he says as he puts it over my eyes.

"But how will I get out there?" I ask.

"Don't worry, I've got you," he says as I feel his hand slip into mine.

We head out onto the porch, and he helps me get down the path, and I can hear the crunch of dirt and rocks beneath my shoe. *Where are they taking me?* I wonder as I can tell we've already passed the cars, but I can't tell what direction we are going.

I hear a creak, and the smell of hay, and I immediately realize we are in the barn. *What did he do? Get me a new saddle?* I ponder as I hear a horse let out a whinny.

"Alright, just one second, okay?" I hear Eli say as he pulls my hand, turns me toward something, and then lets go. I hear him messing around a bit, and then I hear him walk back to me as everyone behind me is giggling and whispering. "You ready?" he asks.

"Yeah, I mean, I think so," I say with a chuckle, and he pulls the bandana off my face.

My eyes flutter open, and I am expecting a saddle or a new bridle since he knows I've been riding the same mare since our Valentine's date. But my heart skips a beat as I see a familiar face staring back at me, her brown eyes seeming to light up as she nickers lightly, and my eyes tear up so bad I can hardly see.

"Laney," I whisper as I begin to sob. "It's my baby, Laney!"

There she is in all her glory, a beautiful red bow around her neck.

"Sure is," Eli says as he rubs my back, and I reach out and touch her velvety nose.

"How did you get her back?" I exclaim, pressing my face against her nose and kissing it, which she seems to welcome with open hooves, appearing to be just as excited as I am.

"I told him who you sold it to," Sparrow says as she steps in next to me with Jade in her arms.

"It wasn't easy, but I got him to part with her once I told him our story and the real reason that you sold her to him," Eli says. "He's got a good heart that one."

"And a deep wallet," Zack says.

"Zack!" Noah scolds him, and I can't help but laugh.

"I can't believe this," I say, and I kiss her nose again before spinning around to look at everyone. "Thank you so much! This is the best Christmas ever."

"We still aren't done," Eli says.

"Huh?" everyone says, looking around the room in surprise.

"You got me more?" I ask.

"One more thing," Eli replies with a smile. "You mind checking her bow?"

"Oh, okay," I say, turning to grab the bow around her neck and begin searching through it, coming up empty. "Sweetheart, there's nothing there—"

I stop short as I glance back to see Eli on one knee, holding a velvet box in his hand—the whole barn has fallen silent.

"Darla, you are my world," Eli begins. "When I met you, I truly was a broken man. . . and then I got messed up again. I couldn't remember what we shared. And that was truly a tragedy."

"Oh my. . ."

"But then I slowly remembered it all, and even when it got scary and hard, or when I needed extra help. . . you never quit on me. You kept showing me love, no matter what, and for that I am the luckiest man in the world," Eli says as he opens the little box. Inside there was a diamond ring, shaped like a lily with little diamond chips down the side. "I learned that life is short, and I don't know how long I have left, but I do know I want to spend the rest of it with you."

"I want to wake up next to you every morning, cradle you in my arms, raise our little farm animals, and have our beautiful, blended family. Not just today, but forever."

"Eli. . ."

"Will you marry me?" Eli asks, and I feel like I can't breathe. I never expected Laney to come back home, but I certainly hadn't ever expected this. *Am I really ready after everything I've been through? What we've been through?*

I only think about it for a moment before I come to a decision.

"Yes," I say tearfully, and Eli slips the ring on my finger. "Just try not to forget about me again, alright?" I joke, and everyone laughs.

"As long as you don't throw any more pies at me," Eli cracks back as he stands up to kiss me.

"You are never going to let me forget that, huh?" I ask before he kisses me again.

"Not as long as we live," Eli says. "Which, God willing, is going to be a long, long time."

Afterword

I hope you enjoyed "Forget Me Not Cowboy," Thank you for supporting me; I appreciate you.

    Stay tuned. More to come!

    Be blessed.

    Skylar

Also By

Trapped with a Navy Seal
https://www.amazon.com/Trapped-Navy-Seal-Enemies-Lovers-ebook/dp/B0CQN7Q6Y3/ref=sr_1_1?crid=19UMLHRRBAWAO&keywords=trapped+with+a+navy+seal+skylar&qid=1707196379&s=digital-text&sprefix=trapped+with+a+nav%2Cdigital-text%2C132&sr=1-1

I never imagined my trip overseas would trap me with a grumpy Navy SEAL.
Losing my sister made me realize life is short.
So, I head for Japan with her eight-year-old son, Alex.
A handsome older Grump sits by us on the airplane.
Alex's fidgeting appears to agitate the Grump.
But Alex's cute face finally wins him over.
Turns out, he is good company.
We land in Japan and say our goodbyes.
So we think.
Alex and I are ready to begin our new life.
Until we meet our new neighbor, Derrick the grump
I don't see much of him.
Until the winds roar and the earth starts to shake.
I panic, thinking of Alex, who is at school.
Trembling, I grasp for the door.
And there he is, Derrick.
A Navy SEAL and protector.
He ushers me to safety on his rooftop.
As a 30-foot tsunami heads towards us.
Trapped together, we share our deepest fears.
The isolation and darkness ignite an indescribable bond between us.

We have to rescue Alex and find a way to safety.

Or our newfound love will never get a chance to blossom.

https://www.amazon.com/Trapped-Navy-Seal-Enemies-Lovers-ebook/dp/B0CQN7Q6Y3/ref=sr_1_1?crid=19UMLHRRBAWAO&keywords=trapped+with+a+navy+seal+skylar&qid=1707196379&s=digital-text&sprefix=trapped+with+a+nav%2Cdigital-text%2C132&sr=1-1

Also By

"Love Unlocked"
An off-limits, innocent ex-con, enemies-to-lovers, clean romance.
https://www.amazon.com/Love-Unlocked-Enemies-Innocent-Ex-ebook
Take a Peak
I refuse to fall in love with an ex-con. Innocent or not.
Ten years in prison and the dominant Abel Delgado is finally home–What did he do?
I have no idea. But I have always considered myself a good Samaritan.
Offering him a job at my deceased father's pizzeria seemed fitting.
Hiring a felon is scary, especially one that is cocky, rigid, and a know it all.
I have a few simple rules: protect the pizzeria and the customers and
watch his every move.

But the more I keep my eyes on him, the more I cannot keep my eyes off him!
His long hair, faded tattoos, and coarse beard demand my attention.

I cannot ignore Abel's masculine and dominant character and his Biceps; let's just say
"he is buff."
I find myself reluctantly yielding to his protection, letting my guard down.
And putting my heart on the line.
Out of nowhere, just like that, heartache and disappointment arise.
Turns out, Abel knows who killed my father.
It has been a mystery all these years, and now I'm forced to relive that terrible day.
It seems like yesterday. Will my heart ever heal from this?
I want to love him enough to see past the pain. The question is, Can I?
https://www.amazon.com/Love-Unlocked-Enemies-Innocent-Ex-ebook
Enjoy!

Also By

Fakin' it with my Firefighter-Contemporary Clean Romance Novel
https://www.amazon.com/Fakin-My-Firefighter-Clean-Romance-ebook/dp/B0CJN8P7HL/ref=sr_1_fkmr1_1?crid=ED2EFXDC

Here is a sneak peek & also, grab your Kleenex!

Falling for a damaged single dad, firefighter, and my brother's best friend was not in the forecast.

Running into the sarcastic Mr. Reed is the last person I desired to see

Instantly, I am reminded of our unpleasant childhood memories and soon realize he is the same OLD Jackson Reed!

So, I thought!

Until I found myself wrapped in his arms amidst of engulfing smoke & fierce flames

The glare and intensity in Jackson's eyes as he carried me out of the raging fire IN-STANTLY

Captured my heart.

We soon discovered falling in love was so easy and felt so right.

But Jackson's "late wife's mother" felt differently!

leaving us with no choice............. A Fake Marriage!

But, after saying "I DO" .... Jackson's hidden secret is revealed, and I question: Am I living

in the Shadows of his past? Is our love strong enough to endure the pain of deception?

Available on KDP and Paperback on Amazon

Fakin' it with my Firefighter-Contemporary Clean Romance Novel
https://www.amazon.com/Fakin-My-Firefighter-Clean-Romance-ebook/dp/B0CJN8P7HL/ref=sr_1_fkmr1_1?crid=ED2EFXDC

Here is a sneak peek & also, grab your Kleenex!

Falling for a damaged single dad, firefighter, and my brother's best friend was not in the forecast.

Running into the sarcastic Mr. Reed is the last person I desired to see
Instantly, I am reminded of our unpleasant childhood memories and soon realize he is the same OLD Jackson Reed!

So, I thought!

Until I found myself wrapped in his arms amidst of engulfing smoke & fierce flames
The glare and intensity in Jackson's eyes as he carried me out of the raging fire IN-STANTLY
Captured my heart.
We soon discovered falling in love was so easy and felt so right.
But Jackson's "late wife's mother" felt differently!
leaving us with no choice............ A Fake Marriage!
But, after saying "I DO" .... Jackson's hidden secret is revealed, and I question: Am I living
in the Shadows of his past? Is our love strong enough to endure the pain of deception?

Available on KDP and Paperback on Amazon

https://www.amazon.com/Fakin-My-Firefighter-Clean-Romance-ebook/dp/B0CJN8P7HL/ref=sr_1_fkmr1_1?crid=ED2EFXDC

Also By

Billionaire Boss & Single Mom

An Instalove Sweet Romance Novel

https://www.amazon.com/Billionaire-Boss-Single-Mom-Instalove-ebook/dp/B0CB72LGXQ/ref=sr_1_1?crid=11JDIHY4CVK8V&keywords=skylar+white+books&qid

Sneak Peek

Leonard is a wholesome billionaire boss who cannot find true love Rayne is a damaged single mom looking for a new start, and love is the last thing on her mind.

She has no money, a failing career, and is exhausted from "life's let-downs." Rayne packs up her

daughter Charlee and heads for LA with her mother, seeking a new start. She lands a temporary

job and unexpectedly finds herself befriending and in love with her Billionaire boss-Leonard.

Who said all billionaires were bad boys?

Leonard is not your ordinary Billionaire; He is Sweet, Single, Compassionate, and Drop Dead Gorgeous but has a problem. Finding the right woman! Until he meets Rayne.

Start Reading Billionaire Boss & Single Mom today!

https://www.amazon.com/Billionaire-Boss-Single-Mom-Instalove-ebook/dp/B0CB72LGXQ/ref=sr_1_1?crid=11JDIHY4CVK8V&keywords=skylar+white+books&qid